Viking Library System
1915 Fir Avenue West
Fergus Falls, MN 56537
218-739-5286

WITHDRAWN

P9-ASG-765

WITHDRAWN

THE LAST RIDE

THE LAST RIDE

ETHAN J. WOLFE

FIVE STAR
A part of Gale, Cengage Learning

GALE
CENGAGE Learning

Farmington Hills, Mich • San Francisco • New York • Waterville, Maine
Meriden, Conn • Mason, Ohio • Chicago

Copyright © 2014 by Ethan J. Wolfe.
Five Star™ Publishing, a part of Gale, Cengage Learning.

ALL RIGHTS RESERVED.
This novel is a work of fiction. Names, characters, places and incidents are either the product of the author's imagination, or, if real, used fictitiously.

No part of this work covered by the copyright herein may be reproduced, transmitted, stored, or used in any form or by any means graphic, electronic, or mechanical, including but not limited to photocopying, recording, scanning, digitizing, taping, Web distribution, information networks, or information storage and retrieval systems, except as permitted under Section 107 or 108 of the 1976 United States Copyright Act, without the prior written permission of the publisher.

The publisher bears no responsibility for the quality of information provided through author or third-party Web sites and does not have any control over, nor assume any responsibility for, information contained in these sites. Providing these sites should not be construed as an endorsement or approval by the publisher of these organizations or of the positions they may take on various issues.

LIBRARY OF CONGRESS CATALOGING-IN-PUBLICATION DATA

Wolfe, Ethan J.
   The last ride / by Ethan J. Wolfe.
     pages cm
     ISBN 978-1-4328-2932-2 (hardcover) — ISBN 1-4328-2932-7
(hardcover)
    I. Title.
PS3612.A5433L37 2014
813'.6—dc23   2014006954

First Edition. First Printing: July 2014
Find us on Facebook– https://www.facebook.com/FiveStarCengage
Visit our website– http://www.gale.cengage.com/fivestar/
Contact Five Star™ Publishing at FiveStar@cengage.com

Printed in the United States of America
1 2 3 4 5 6 7 18 17 16 15 14

This one is for the East Coast Cowgirl, a great friend and colleague

CHAPTER ONE

San Francisco 1860

Walking along a sidewalk made of plank wood, Walter Burke tried to think of a word to describe San Francisco. Years earlier, when he attended school in the one-room schoolhouse back home, Miss Purdy, his teacher, spoke of such places. Cities, she called them. Giant towns, really, where a great many people came together to live and work. This San Francisco certainly qualified as such, although a proper word to describe it still escaped him because his vocabulary wasn't that good, so said Miss Purdy. He hoped to make it better one day by reading books and newspapers.

With his younger sister Joanna by his side, Walter paused at a street corner to allow several horse-drawn carriages the right of way. A few men on horseback rode with the carriages, but they wore city clothing: frock coats, fancy white shirts and tall hats. It was a mystery to Walter why a man would dress such a way to ride a horse. Another thing he noticed, too, was the lack of firearms among the men. Not a pistol or rifle in sight. Maybe in such a big town there was no need. There seemed to be an oil lamp mounted atop a post every twenty feet along the streets. Maybe the city was so well lit at night, a man could walk the streets after dark and not fear a bushwhacker.

The street cleared.

"Best give me your hand, Jo," Walter said.

"I'm fourteen, Walter," Joanna said. "I'm not a baby anymore."

"I know you're not a baby," Walter said. "Don't you think I know that? Give me your hand, anyway."

Joanna stuck out her hand and Walter took hold of it tightly. Together, they crossed the widest street either of them had ever seen.

When they reached the other side of the street, they unlocked hands and paused while Walter dug a handbill from his shirt pocket and unfolded it. He studied the handbill for a moment.

"It must be around here somewhere."

"Walter, look," Joanna said, pointing a finger.

Walter turned and looked where Joanna was pointing. Not very far away was the Bay of San Francisco, with several four-mast schooner ships towering above the water.

"I do believe one of them is yours," Walter said. "We'll go find out as soon as I take care of my business. Then we go see about that boardinghouse for tonight."

"I still don't see why I can't stay with you, Walter."

"I told you why a hundred times, Jo," Walter said. "I promised Pa, and that's all there is to the subject. I won't break no promise. Now be quiet and let me get my bearings."

Walter studied the handbill. It told him nothing, because he knew nothing of San Francisco. He could be standing right in front of the building he was looking for and not know it from any other building, they were all so big. Four to six windows high, some of them, and wide as two barns put together.

Why did people need so much room?

"Walter, look."

"What now?" Walter snapped.

A wagon rode past them in the street. The wagon was pulled by a lone mule. The man riding in the buckboard seemed in no hurry, nor did the mule. On both sides of the wagon were baskets full of fruits and vegetables. At the corner, the man stopped the wagon and stepped down to the street.

"Today's fruits fresh from market!" the man yelled. "All kinds, ready ripe to sell!"

People along the streets suddenly veered toward the wagon.

"You ever see anything like that, Walter?"

"No."

"Can we take a look?"

"What for?"

"I want to see, that's what for."

Joanna stepped down into the dirty street and walked carefully to avoid the horse chips that seemed to be everywhere and stopped with the crowd at the wagon. Within seconds, Walter was by her side.

"What is that?" Joanna asked, pointing to a basket full of oblong-shaped fruits.

"I don't know," Walter said. "I recognize the apples, potatoes, corn and carrots. All them others, I don't know."

The man was loading apples into a paper sack for a woman. When he was done, Joanna tugged on his elbow.

"Those in the basket there, what are those?" Joanna asked.

"Those are Bartlett pears, miss," the man said.

"Are they good?" Joanna asked.

"Very sweet and juicy," the man said.

"How much for one?"

"Two cents," the man said.

Joanna looked at Walter.

Walter sighed. He dug out four cents and handed it to the man.

"Do you want a bag?" the man said.

"What for?" asked Walter.

Joanna took the two pears and she and Walter returned to the sidewalk. Joanna immediately bit into her pear.

"It's good, Walter. Juicy like the man said."

Walter took a bite of his. "By God, it is," he said. "Now let's find this building before next winter sets in."

Walter and Joanna walked a few more blocks, but neither of them had any idea where they were or where they were going. The city was just too large and confusing for them to figure out without some help.

At an intersection, Walter took out the handbill to study it again. There was a basket on the corner filled with trash and he and Joanna tossed in the remains of the pears.

"Walter, that man there looks like a sheriff," Joanna said. "Maybe he can help?"

The man walking toward them on the wood sidewalk was dressed in a heavy blue uniform of some type. A tall hat with leather trim perched on his head. A thick leather belt held a Navy Colt revolver in a flap holster. He carried a stick with a leather loop through which his right hand was placed. He twirled the stick as he walked. A shiny brass star was pinned to the right side of the blue jacket.

"I believe you're right, Jo," Walter said.

Walter and Joanna approached the man.

"Excuse me, mister, my sister and me are looking for this address. Maybe you know where it's at?"

Walter showed the man the handbill.

"You're not far from it," the man said. He used the stick to point. "Walk three blocks that way, then turn left and go until you reach the waterfront. You'll find it there along the street opposite the piers."

"Thank you," Walter said.

"Are you a sheriff?" asked Joanna.

"No, miss," the man said. "I'm a member of the San Francisco Police Department."

Walter and Joanna watched the man walk away and turn the

corner at the end of the block.

"What's a police department, Walter?"

"I think it's like a bunch of deputies in the city," Walter said. "Come on, let's go."

Holding Joanna's hand, Walter followed the man's directions and walked three blocks, turned left and walked another few blocks to the waterfront.

There, Walter and Joanna paused because they had never seen such confusion in all their lives. First off, the wide street opposite the bay was made of stones set in quick dry cement. Horse-drawn wagons and carriages were everywhere, mostly hauling freight from the ships anchored off the wharf. Freight offices lined the street to their backs. Piano music came from somewhere. Men sold hot and cold food in wagons along the street. It seemed to them that everybody was talking all at once and nobody was listening to a word being said.

And of course, directly in front of them anchored in the bay were the majestic schooner ships.

"Looks like we can kill two birds with one stone," Walter said.

"What do you mean, Walter?"

"Once I see about this job, we don't have far to go to see about your ship," Walter said, and pointed to the ships.

"Hey, look," Joanna said. "That's it right there."

Not four storefronts to their left was the address on the handbill. They walked to the office and read the large poster out front.

Pony Express Recruitment Center

Young, skinny, wiry fellows wanted. Must be willing to risk death daily to deliver the U.S. Mail. Pay is one hundred dollars a month. Apply inside.

"Come inside with me, but wait by the door," Walter said.

Walter opened the door and he and Joanna entered the office. It was sparsely furnished with a counter, a woodstove, a few oil lamps and a desk. A man wearing a suit stood behind the counter.

Walter approached the counter and set the handbill on the smooth wood top.

"I want to sign up to be a rider like it says here," Walter said.

The man studied Walter for a long moment. "You look kind of tall, son. How tall are you?"

"I don't rightly know," Walter said. "I ain't been measured since the first grade."

"You look lean enough," the man said. "How much do you weigh?"

"I can't say for certain," Walter said. "Last year, I stepped on a rusty nail and I saw the doctor in town and he said I weighed a hundred and thirty pounds. He figured that when I stood on this metal platform."

The man nodded his head. "Can you ride one hundred miles a day?"

"I broke horses on my Pa's spread since I'm twelve years old," Walter said. "I can ride a hundred miles or more all right."

"Are you proficient with firearms?"

"What's proficient?"

"Can you shoot a long gun and a pistol and can you do so on horseback?"

"I can," Walter said. "Half the time it was the only way to feed ourselves."

"You understand the risk that comes with delivering the U.S. Mail?"

"I do, sir," Walter said. "But, I need to make that hundred dollars a month. You see, my parents are both gone now and I'm sending my young sister there to live with my Pa's sister in New York. I guess they call that an aunt. She's going to see to it my sister gets a proper education and that hundred dollars a month will help pay for that."

The man looked at Joanna in the corner.

"I see," the man said. "Can you read and write your name?"

"My schooling went to the sixth grade," Walter said. "After that, my Pa needed me on the ranch, but I can read decent enough and write a fair amount."

"Read this," the man said and produced the San Francisco newspaper from under the counter. "That first story and headline."

Walter looked at the newspaper. It was unlike any newspaper he'd ever seen in that it was so thick and double-folded. He looked at the first story on the page.

"Congress un . . . able to reach agree . . . ment on issue of slavery and se . . . se . . . cession," Walter said. "With the im . . . pending election just . . ."

"That's fine, son," the man said. "Report here tomorrow morning at seven. We'll get you started then."

"I have to see my sister off first," Walter said. "Her ship sails for New York at first light. It's just right across the street."

The man nodded. "I'm Horace Wright, agent for the U.S. Mail Service."

"Walter Burke. That's my sister Joanna," Walter said.

"I'll see you right after she sets sail," Wright said.

"Yes, sir," Walter said.

Walter and Joanna left the office and stood on the cobblestone street for a moment to get their bearings.

"Let's see about your ticket first, then let's get our bags from the stage office," Walter said. "Then we'll see about that boardinghouse for tonight."

Holding hands, Walter and Joanna crossed the wide cobblestone street to the wharf where the massive ships were anchored.

"Which one is mine?"

"The one going to New York City," Walter said.

13

CHAPTER TWO

Mrs. Oudin ran the boardinghouse from her large home a few blocks from the bay area. She was a big, plump woman of middle age, who took to boarding guests after her husband passed away some fifteen years ago. She ran a clean house, served two meals, breakfast and supper, appropriately priced at twenty-five cents for breakfast and fifty cents for supper, a nickel extra if you took your meals in your room.

There were twelve rooms for guests of which half were double occupancy. Walter and Joanna took a room with two beds for a dollar and twenty-five cents for the night.

As Walter set three bags on the floor between the two beds, he said, "Glad we're only staying the night. At these prices, I'll be busted out inside a week."

At supper, the table was set for twelve. Except for Mrs. Oudin and Joanna, the remaining guests for supper were men. The meal consisted of chicken dumplings in gravy, fresh baked bread, coffee, milk or water, with apple pie for dessert for an extra nickel. Walter thought fifty cents a high price for some flour, grease and chicken stuffing, but it, along with the bread, filled his belly pretty well. He also thought ten cents was outright robbery for two slices of pie, but seeing as he wouldn't see Joanna for many years probably, he reluctantly parted with the dime.

During supper the men spoke mostly of the War Between the States that was sure to come within the next year. A few of the men said the issue was resolving slavery, that no man had the right to claim another as property. Others at the table said the more important issue was preserving the nation, that a nation divided would surely fall as history proved time and again. Someone mentioned the Roman Empire as an example, and someone else said what happened to the Romans would never happen in America because America believed in freedom. Then someone else said the freedom was only if your skin was white and an argument broke out that Mrs. Oudin had to quiet.

Walter had only a vague notion of what the men were talking about and kept his tongue to himself, except to ask Mrs. Oudin for extra bread. Joanna sat to Mrs. Oudin's left and the two engaged in conversation the entire time food was on the table, although Walter couldn't hear what about over the voices of the men.

After supper, the men went to the parlor to smoke cigars and drink brandy. Walter and Joanna retreated to their room on the third floor of the house.

Walter sat on his bed, opened his large bag and started checking his gear. Joanna sat on her bed and started to cry softly.

"What?"

"You're sending me away tomorrow, Walter."

"I'm not sending you away, Jo," Walter said. "This is what Pa wanted for you and our aunt is kin. Maybe the only kin we have left. She'll see to it you get a proper education and home. I can't give you neither and you know that. Pa knew that. That's why he made me promise."

Joanna wiped her eyes and stood up. "I have to use the privacy."

"Well, hurry up," Walter said. "We have to get to sleep right quick."

Joanna went to the door and left it open as she went out to search for the privacy.

Walter tossed his bag aside and flopped down onto the pillow. It was nobody's fault, it was just the way things turned out. Truth be told, James Burke, their father, was an eastern dude out of New Jersey. He came west in 1838 and settled in Oregon to work for the Army. There was talk of a cross-country trail for settlers to follow and the Army needed outposts and horses. An Army afoot is useless, his Pa said. With what little money he saved back east, James bought a small spread where he captured and bred horses for the Army. Two years later, he met and married Joann Wilson. A year later, Walter was born. Two children died in childbirth before Joanna came along in forty-six. There wasn't a lot growing up. The Army didn't exactly make folks rich, but there always seemed to be just enough with what Ma grew and Pa hunted to supplement the Army money.

By the time he was ten, Walter could rope and ride as well as most men. When he turned twelve, his father gave him an old plains rifle and taught him to shoot. It wasn't long after that Walter was the main hunter in the family, which freed up his Pa's time for horse training.

Of course, Joann being his mother and a woman, she insisted Walter attend school in town whenever they had a teacher available and it was in session. Although he'd much rather be out hunting or training a horse with Pa, Walter was grateful he did have some schooling because he was starting to understand how important reading and writing was in the world if a man was to make his mark.

The winter Joanna turned seven, their mother took sick with what the town doctor called influenza. It was a cold and wet winter that year and the influenza grew worse, into what the doctor called pneumonia.

They buried Joann Burke early in the spring.

Her passing took the life right out of James Burke. He lasted another seven years, but there was no joy in his life anymore, no desire to build the ranch or succeed in business, or even train horses for the Army. He did these things, but it seemed to Walter his Pa was simply going through the motions of doing what he had to and there was no joy in doing them.

While breaking a mustang, James fell off his horse and lay where he fell for several hours until Walter came in from hunting and found him. The doctor said it was something called a heart attack. James regained consciousness long enough to tell Walter his final wishes. There was a legal piece of paper in his chest called a will. James passed that night in his sleep. He was forty-three years old.

In the coming months, Walter found out just how bad things were. Years' worth of back taxes owed the government, plus newer, larger ranches in the area and along the Oregon Trail, gave Walter little choice but to sell the property, pay off the taxes and use what little money was left to send Joanna to New York as their father wished on his death bed.

"Walter?" Joanna asked softly.

Walter opened his eyes and looked at Joanna.

"I'm never gonna see you again, am I?"

"Course you will," Walter said. "Maybe not for a while, but when you least expect it, I'll be there. I'll dance at your wedding."

"Promise."

"With all my heart."

Joanna smiled and sat on her bed. "Can I see that map one more time?"

"You can take it with you," Walter said. He removed the folded map from his bag and spread it out on the bed. "Mark off the stops along the way to show your kids one day."

Joanna sat next to him and looked at the faded map.

"We are here," Walter said and placed his finger on San Francisco. "And you are going here to New York City." With his finger, he traced a path down the coast of California to Mexico, along South America, then north along the Americas' coast all the way to New York City.

Joanna looked up from the map at Walter. "It's a long way, Walter."

"Yes, it is," Walter said. "Almost three months at sea."

"What am I supposed to do all that time?"

"I expect mostly talk with the other people traveling with you," Walter said. "But I got you something for the trip. Cost me a dollar and ten cents."

"What?" asked Joanna, her face suddenly lit with the thought of a gift.

Walter dug out the leather-covered book he purchased at the general store back home and gave it to Joanna. She immediately opened it. All the pages were blank.

"Walter, they ain't no words in the book," Joanna said.

"I know that," Walter said. "This here is called a journal. What you do, see, is every day you write in this here book what you do every day you're on ship. Like keeping a record of your adventures. I got you some pencils, enough to last the trip, but if they don't, I'm sure you can buy some on board."

Joanna hugged the book tightly to her chest. "Thank you, Walter. I will write in it every day. I promise."

"All right, let's go to bed," Walter said. "Daylight comes early and that ship ain't gonna wait on us if we're late."

"Turn around while I put on my sleeping clothes."

"Like I didn't powder your bottom when you was a baby," Walter said.

"I ain't no baby no more, Walter," Joanna said. "I'm practically a grown woman."

Walter grinned at Joanna as he turned his back to her. "I expect that you are," he said.

CHAPTER THREE

Standing on the boardwalk, looking up at the ship, Walter thought it the biggest manmade thing he'd ever seen. He understood nothing about ships, why they stayed afloat or how they stayed on course, but he knew that ship could sail around the world and back and be no worse for wear just by looking at it.

Joanna hugged him tightly. He had to pry her loose.

"That man up there is yelling for all aboard," Walter said. "You best be going."

Joanna released her hold on Walter and nodded. She was too choked up to speak.

"Go on, now," Walter said. "I'll watch till you get on board."

Joanna nodded and stepped into the long line of boarding passengers. Walter stood watching until she reached the top, looked down at him and blew him a kiss. Then she was gone.

Walter felt a tear roll down his cheek and he wiped it away with the back of his hand. It would not sit well with his new boss the first day on the job to pin him as a crybaby.

His emotions under control, Walter crossed the wide cobblestone street and entered the Pony Express office. Horace Wright was behind the counter. He looked up when Walter entered.

"Morning, Walter," Wright said. "Your sister get off all right?"

"Yes, sir," Walter said. "Just a few minutes ago."

"Good. Do you have any gear?"

"One bag back at the boardinghouse," Walter said. "Mrs. Oudin is watching it for me until I pick it up."

Wright grinned. "I know Mrs. Oudin," he said. "Did she charge you a nickel to watch your bag?"

"Not yet."

"She will," Wright said. "Get your bag and report back here. You have papers to fill out. Can you use pen and ink without making a mess?"

"Learned it in school."

"Good. Some other men should be here by the time you return," Wright said. "You'll all ride by coach to your home station."

Walter left the office and walked the quarter mile to Mrs. Oudin's boardinghouse. Mr. Wright was correct, she charged him a nickel for holding his bag. He found her in the kitchen where she was having tea and where she charged him the nickel.

"Did your sister board her ship without incident?" Mrs. Oudin asked.

"Yes, ma'am," Walter said.

"Would you care for a cup of my special tea, Mr. Burke?"

"I would, but I don't have the time," Walter said. "I start my new job as a rider for the Pony Express this morning."

"You'll be a long time in the saddle, Mr. Burke," Mrs. Oudin said. "For a member of the Pony Express, I'll knock fifty cents off my usual rate of two dollars."

"Well, ma'am, like I said, I don't have the time," Walter said, thinking two dollars for a cup of tea the most extravagant thing he'd ever heard of. He didn't even like tea, much less pay that kind of money for some hot water and dried leaves.

He left with his forty-pound bag slung over his back and walked the streets thinking two dollars would buy steaks for a week, much less a cup of tea. At the Pony Express office, he carried his bag inside and set it down in the corner by the door.

"Mrs. Oudin charge you a nickel for the bag?" Wright asked.

"She did and something else," Walter said. "She offered me a cup of tea for two dollars a cup. I never heard of tea costing more than a steak dinner."

Wright stared at Walter for a moment.

"Walter, Mrs. Oudin is a . . . were there any female guests at supper last night?"

"Just my sister."

"That's because those men . . . Walter, Mrs. Oudin is what we call a sporting woman," Wright said. "The two dollars ain't for no tea. It's for her private company."

"That's what she meant by the saddle?"

Wright grinned. "Come out back and sign the papers. You can meet the other boys you'll be traveling with to the Wyoming Territory outpost."

Behind the counter was a separate room with five small tables and chairs, of which three were occupied. Each man looked up from their papers to look at Walter.

"Let's see," Wright said. "Oh, hell, just introduce yourselves. Take that seat with pen and ink and fill out your name where asked."

Walter nodded and took the chair. He picked up the paper and started to read it when the man to his left spoke up and broke his concentration.

"You can read that, or you just funning?" he asked.

Walter turned to his left. The man was no older than him, but smaller in height, although they appeared to be of the same frame. "Yes, I can," Walter said.

"My name is Sweetwater Leon, and I told Mr. Wright I can read, but I really can only read my name and a few ABCs and some numbers," Sweetwater said.

"I can read," the man to Walter's right said. "Says we agreeing to be members of the Pony Express as part of the U.S.

Postal Service, and that we hold them without blame if an Indian kills us or we fall off our horse and git kilt."

Walter looked to his right. The man, a boy really, maybe fifteen at most, was a runt of a thing, but the look in his eyes said he believed he was a giant. Walter saw that look before in runts. They were always ready to fight at the slightest cross word to prove they weren't small in courage.

"Name is William Cody, but nobody calls me nothing but Bill," he said.

Walter looked past Bill to the lean, hawkish-looking fellow to Bill's left. "And who are you?" Walter said.

"Name is Johnson," he said.

"What's your Christian name?" Walter asked.

"People call me Slicker," he said.

"Why is that, because you're smart?" Walter said. "Or hard to get hold of?"

"Well, what's your name?" Slicker asked.

"Walter Burke, and seeing as how we'll be doing some traveling together, it's best we get off on the right foot as friends," Walter said.

"I can write my name," Sweetwater said.

Walter turned to Sweetwater. "You're none too smart in the head, are you, Sweetwater?"

Wright came into the back room. "Your stage leaves in ten minutes. I'll need those papers," he said.

They signed the papers, even Sweetwater, then met Mr. Wright out front where a stagecoach was at the ready, with driver and armed lookout.

"Good luck, boys," Wright said.

The four of them entered the coach and took seats. Walter placed his bag between his legs and looked out the window. "I guess it will be a while before we see a big town like this again," he said.

"I don't care if I never see a big town ever again," Slicker said.

"No?" Walter said.

"I'm gonna have a spread of my own one day," Slicker said. "As far away from a big city as I can find."

"I like big cities," Bill said. "I lived in Leavenworth with my folks for a time. Until they stabbed my pa and I ran off to work for a freight company as a messenger boy cause I can run fast."

"Stabbed your pa? Who stabbed your pa, what for?"

"Makin' speeches in the public square," Bill said.

"Makin' speeches?" Walter asked. "What kinda speeches?"

"Against slavery," Bill said. "He was saying how it ain't right for one man to own another and some men who didn't take kindly to his words stabbed him. He died when I was but eleven."

"I agree with your pa," Walter said. "Sounds like your pa was a brave man."

"Back home in Oregon, all they talk about is war," Slicker said. "The north against the south. They say they'll be fighting inside a year."

"You thinking a joining the Army?" Sweetwater asked.

"And fight for what?" asked Slicker. "We ain't even in the Union."

"I'd go," Bill said. "For the north on account of what them slave owners did to my pa. I'd kill a bunch of them fer sure."

"You boys go off and fight a war a country away if you want to," Walter said. "I can't afford to git killed until my little sister is a proper grown woman."

"You got a sister?" Sweetwater asked.

"Put her on a ship bound for New York this morning," Walter said. "She's going to live with my aunt and go to school. That's where most of my pay will be going as it's my obligation to take care of her until she's grown."

23

"What's girls need with schooling?"

"Maybe out here a body can get by with being able to write their name, but I hear back east people work in offices and reading is mighty important," Walter said.

The stagecoach reached the city limits and the scenery slowly changed to countryside. The four quieted down for a while as they watched city become country and country become open range.

Walter thought about Joanna on that giant ship. She was a brave girl, as brave as any man he knew, but all that time at sea, and alone to boot, it worried him just a bit. A few years back, she was maybe eleven; he and Pa were tending a horse in the corral. Joanna hung on the fence, watching, like she always did, but then when he looked over, she was gone. He figured she made a trip to the privacy or went into the house for something. A little while later, he happened to glance toward the ridge that overlooked their property and spotted Joanna standing there in the field maybe five hundred yards out. She was just standing there, looking up at the ridge where three Indians on horseback were looking down on her. He saddled a horse and raced out to her, grabbed her by the arm and tossed her behind him on the saddle. He scolded her and asked her what she thought she was doing. She wanted to see what them Indians were looking at, she said, without any fear for her safety. What they was looking at is you, he told her. She said she hoped they got a good look and liked what they saw.

Sometimes bravery is the same as foolishness, Walter concluded.

On a long journey in close quarters, there is nothing else to do except talk and in the coming days and nights, Walter got to know his fellow travelers right well. They talked or napped during the day when the stagecoach bumped them around over rough ground, then talked some more when they spent the night at a way station.

For instance, he learned that Sweetwater Leon was born on the Sweetwater River in Wyoming Territory not far from where their destination was located. His folks were traveling to Colorado Territory when Sweetwater decided to be born and they named him for the river he took his first breath upon.

To call Sweetwater dim-witted would not be truthful. He was slow thinking, couldn't read worth a lick, but he held his own in a conversation if given the time to think about his words before speaking them.

Slicker Johnson, on the other hand, could read and write and was quick with his tongue and his wits. His real name was Ned, but it was so long since anybody called him that he sometimes forgot and only remembered when asked. His pa took to calling him Slicker or Slick when he was just ten and displayed an excellent ability with racing ponies. Slick in the saddle, his pa would say. He figured that ability would come in right handy riding for the Pony Express.

Bill Cody, on the other hand and despite being just a runt, talked the big talk of a man with his sights set upon great things. He ran his tongue constantly, bragging how one day he would be the most famous man in America, more famous even than the President. Walter believed the runt, for he had such persuading ways about him, he made you believe every word he told you, even if upon reflection it was nonsense.

It was many days in the stagecoach before they arrived at their destination, Fort Laramie in Wyoming Territory.

Walter had seen Army posts before, but none quite this size and with so many men assigned to it. Used to protect settlers moving west, two hundred soldiers patrolled the frontier in search of danger, oftentimes escorting settlers for many miles.

Once inside the gate, the stagecoach driver let them off in front of the Pony Express office. The interior of the fort was bustling with activity. Soldiers were everywhere, walking, working, practicing their drills. A large blacksmith shop was manned by a massive man who pounded out shoes on an anvil.

A man came out of the office and introduced himself as Mr. Hill to his four new men. "Come in the office where I'll acquaint you with how things will operate. There's hot coffee on the woodstove."

They followed Mr. Hill into the office where it was warmer than the chilly April air outside. There was a desk and a long table in the office and on the table was a large, detailed map of the United States and its territories.

"Grab your coffee and gather round," Mr. Hill said.

They filled tin cups with hot coffee and gathered around the map. Sketched in black ink, the route was drawn in red ink to make it easier to read.

"There are 184 outposts on the route, ten to twenty miles apart," Mr. Hill said. "Each man will ride seventy-five to one hundred miles a day on your given route. You will carry one mochila, or mail pouch, loaded with twenty pounds of mail."

Mr. Hill picked up a doubled-sided, leather saddlebag with a leather strip between the two pouches. "You sling it over your saddle and sit on the strap, securing the bags to your horse. To keep things light, you will carry one canteen, jerked meat, a revolver and, if you choose to, a bible. You may carry tobacco and paper in your pockets if so desired."

Mr. Hill opened one bag and produced four brand new Pony Express messenger badges and gave one to each man. Walter looked at the badge. It was shaped funny and came to a point on the bottom. A rider on horse was centered on the badge and it was topped with a sitting eagle with spread wings.

"You wear this at all times you're on duty," Mr. Hill said.

"Now, look at the map. The trail starts in St. Joseph, Missouri, and ends in Sacramento, California. There it gits on a steamer bound for San Francisco. Any questions?"

They had questions, but held their tongues for fear of looking slow or foolish in each other's eyes.

"All right, then," Mr. Hill said. "You leave for the outposts first light tomorrow. You can sleep in the bunk room out back tonight. The Army serves evening chow at 5:30. Don't be late or these Army boys will bite your fingers off for an extra slice of bread."

Mr. Hill turned away from the table and then paused to look back. "And I hope the four of you are orphans," he said.

With several hours to kill before supper, they filed into the bunk house and chose their beds for the night. Walter sat on his chosen bed and opened his gear bag to dig out his Colt 1851 revolver. He started to clean it when Sweetwater sat on the bed next to him.

"Walter, what that Mr. Hill said about carrying a revolver," Sweetwater said. "I ain't got one."

Walter looked up from his cleaning. "I expect you can get one at the Army store."

"I ain't got no twenty dollars to buy it," Sweetwater said.

Bill opened his gear bag and produced a belt with two holsters. "I got me two of them," he said. "Belonged to my pa and now they belong to me."

"I got a Dragoon," Slicker said and produced the massive Colt revolver from his gear bag. "Shoots a .44 ball, though none too accurate. It packs a big wallop, though, if it hits you."

"By God, Slick, you can hammer horseshoes with that piece," Walter said.

"What am I supposed to do, Walter?" Sweetwater asked.

"The one thing I didn't sell of my pa's was his two Colt revolvers," Walter said. He dug the second one out of the bag

27

and handed it to Sweetwater. "Shoots a .36 ball, but ain't heavy like the Dragoon. You can borrow it, powder and balls until you can buy your own."

"Thanks, Walter," Sweetwater said.

"Just don't shoot your foot off," Walter said. "Trigger's a mite sensitive once it's cocked."

"Why do you suppose Mr. Hill said we should carry a bible?" Slicker said.

"I expect if you fall off your horse and break your neck, your last words might be something from the Good Book," Walter said.

"Well, I ain't got one," Slicker said.

"Me, neither," Bill said.

"I gave mine to my sister," Walter said.

"I got one," Sweetwater said. "Belonged to my ma."

"Let me see it," Walter said.

Sweetwater dug through his gear bag and produced an old faded copy of the Old Testament. He handed it to Walter.

"It's a fine old bible, Sweet," Walter said. "Maybe one day I'll teach you to read from it."

"Just having it is enough," Sweetwater said.

"I expect so," Walter said.

CHAPTER FOUR

Walter rose from his bunk while it was still dark and took coffee on the porch to watch the sunrise. He brought his tobacco pouch and paper to roll a smoke while he drank his coffee and waited for the cook to make breakfast.

Six months of riding seventy-five to a hundred miles a day hardened his body so that his frame was all lean hard muscle. The first few days in the saddle, his back ached and his legs cramped so bad, he swore he'd never walk again. After a few weeks, he didn't give it a second thought.

Walter struck a wood match against the wood post of the porch and lit his smoke. In the distance, the first morning light gave pale color to the countryside, reddish and orange, mostly. This Wyoming was mighty pretty country, especially at sunrise and set, he thought as he watched the sun slowly rise.

As he smoked and sipped coffee, Walter could smell bacon cooking in the fry pan. His stomach rumbled just smelling it and the fresh biscuits he knew were baking in the oven.

"Hey, Walter, git a move on, boy," Boss yelled from the open window. "Daylight's a burning."

Walter tossed the cigarette and went inside the shack.

Boss ran things at the outpost. A big man, twenty years Walter's senior, Boss was the sort of man who never stopped working so long as the sun was up. He saw to it the wranglers took proper care of the horses, made sure supplies were plentiful, kept the scouts on their toes for Indian raids and, most importantly, handled all the mail and correspondence for the riders. If there was nothing else to do, he would chop wood or find some other chore to do to busy his time. Today, it was just Walter. Some days, as much as three men slept over. Often-times, it was Slicker and Sweetwater, who were becoming good, close friends, but today, it was just him.

Boss's rule, the rider ate first. Walter sat down to a plate of bacon, beans, fried eggs and biscuits. He sipped coffee while he ate and listened to Boss's latest news. Boss took coffee while he spoke.

"I hear tell little William Cody made a ride of 322 miles in twenty-one hours," Boss said. "Took twenty-one horses to make the trip. Between Red Butts and Rocky Ridge on account of his relief was killed by Paiutes."

"I thought they was done with warring," Walter said.

"A bunch of them broke away and is causing all kinds a problems," Boss said. "You keep a sharp eye on your run today. A raiding party has been spotted on the ridges along the route."

"I always keep a sharp eye," Walter said.

"So did Bob Haslam, and look what happened to him," Boss said.

Robert Haslam, the rider who would later deliver Lincoln's inaugural address, was shot with a Paiute arrow through the jaw, losing three teeth.

"I'll keep my eyes open, Boss," Walter said. "And my Colt in my belt."

"I wish I could give you the Henry rifle, but it's the only one we got, Walter," Boss said.

Walter nodded as he finished his coffee. The Henry rifle Boss spoke of was the new rifle manufactured by the New Haven Arms Company, designed by Ben Henry. It was a lever action rifle that held sixteen rounds of self-contained .44 cartridges, a new and experimental round in firearms. If a rider coming in was being chased by Indians or robbers, one Henry could ward off the bunch. Walter's Colt was cap and ball and if the powder got wet it wouldn't fire. Walter understood that a self-contained cartridge was waterproof, though he'd never had the opportunity to fire one.

"Any more talk of the war?" Walter asked.

"Ah, those big bellies in Washington, all they do is talk and talk and eat and eat," Boss said. "The South is claiming secession, the North wants to stay unified, but with freed slaves. Newspapers say Lincoln will win the election and if that happens, war will surely follow. Why, you thinking of joining up?"

"No, sir," Walter said. "Not for no eleven dollars a month. I send my sister ninety a month from my pay. She's in what they call finishing school back east."

"What's finishing school?" Boss asked.

"I'm not rightly sure," Walter said. "I think it's school where they teach girls how to be proper women."

A wrangler poked his head through the door. "Hey, Walter, your mustang's saddled and ready to go," he said.

Walter stood up. He grabbed his loaded Colt revolver off his bunk and tucked it in his belt. "See you on the return, Boss. Who's coming through tonight?"

"I believe it's Sweetwater," Boss said.

"Tell him hey for me if I got no return mail," Walter said. He grabbed the mochila by the door and went outside where the saddled mustang waited. Back east, riders rode thoroughbreds where the terrain was kinder on the horse, but here the country was too rugged for so delicate an animal.

Walter slung the mochila over the specially designed, lightweight saddle, then climbed aboard. With a wave to the wrangler, he was off and running.

The mustang could reach speeds of thirty-five miles an hour, but there was no need for that at the moment. Walter had seven stops to make today, covering a distance of nearly eighty miles, so he kept the mustang moving at a steady pace of around twenty miles an hour by his estimate.

Things went as usual the first five stops. With each stop came a fresh mustang, a sip of water and maybe a piece of jerked meat or a biscuit. On the fifth run, he spotted Paiute pony soldiers dogging him. They stayed back a quarter mile on his left flank. They were in no hurry, but the message was clear. They were a long way from home and it wasn't to hunt mule deer or bison.

Walter upped the gait to a full-blown run and kept the mustang moving all out for ten or more miles to the sixth stop. Two wranglers met him at the gate.

"Some pony soldiers are dogging me," Walter said as he dismounted.

"We seen them," a wrangler said. "Want us to ride out with the Henry and scatter them off?"

"That's what they want," Walter said as he jumped aboard the fresh mustang. "An excuse to start slinging arrows. I'll be all right."

The seventh stop covered a distance of thirteen miles. Walter needed to bust the mustang loose and ride full out the entire distance. While he stopped to remount, the Paiute dog soldiers rode on and then came in from the west to close the gap between them and Walter.

They had no firearms, but their arrows could hit what they aimed at from a distance of two hundred yards. Walter's Colt could not, having an effective range of fifty feet at best. Plus, the arrows were silent, so you had no warning one was coming.

Walter dug his spurs in and pushed the mustang for all it had, but it wasn't enough. Several Paiute soldiers that had ridden on ahead and now backtracked on his flank were gaining and there was no way to outrun them on a long stretch.

The first arrows flew past his head and Walter ducked down low in the saddle to avoid a second one. He was halfway through the run and there was no way to fend them off if they were determined to make a go of it.

Then he felt a sting in his upper back on the left side. For a moment, Walter didn't realize he'd been shot by an arrow until he saw his blood on the mane of the mustang, then he saw the arrowhead sticking out of his chest.

Strange how it didn't hurt. He knew the excitement of the moment prevented him from thinking about the pain. To his left, Walter spotted a dog soldier coming up fast, his tomahawk at the ready.

Walter drew the Colt with his right hand, cocked the hammer and fired a .36-caliber ball directly into the dog soldier's chest. He was the first man Walter ever killed. He stuck the Colt back in his belt, put his head down and rode as hard and fast as the mustang would allow him.

With the stop in sight, Walter felt things go hazy and he knew he was blacking out. He wrapped the reins around his wrists and put his head down and felt his eyes close.

He heard rifle shots.

Then it all went black.

When Walter opened his eyes again, he was shirtless on the table inside the cabin at the stop. Two wranglers turned him on his side and pressed their weight down on him. The shack boss, Mr. Harvey, said, "Hold him tight now. Get that rag in his mouth."

A towel was placed between Walter's teeth as Harvey broke the arrow off at the shaft a few inches from Walter's back.

"Now, Walter, you bite hard," Harvey said as he used the butt of his revolver to smack the arrow clear through Walter's back until it came out of his chest.

CHAPTER FIVE

When Walter opened his eyes next, he was in bed inside the cabin. His chest was bandaged and ached something terrible and a fierce thirst gripped his throat. He forced himself to sit up and just the effort of doing so made the room spin around in a dizzying circle.

Before Walter could stand, the door opened and Harvey walked in, followed closely by Sweetwater.

"Where you going?" Harvey asked.

"Not very far, that's for sure," Walter said. "But I could use some water."

Sweetwater went to the water bucket on the table and filled a tin cup. "Here you go, Walt," he said and gave the cup to Walter.

Walter downed the cup in several long swallows. "By God, I'm thirsty," he said.

"You been out for three and a half days, you ought to be," Sweetwater said.

"Want some grub?" Harvey asked.

"Yeah," Walter said as he flopped back down onto the bed.

"I'll get the boys to rustle you up something," Harvey said and left the cabin.

"How's it feel, Walter?" Sweetwater asked. "Your wound."

"Like I been shot clean through with an arrow. How do you think it feels? It hurts," Walter said. "Who doctored me up?"

"Harvey," Sweetwater said. "He had some schooling back east. He pushed the arrow clean through, then cleaned the wound with rye whiskey. When he got the bleeding to stop, he . . . I forget the fancy word, but what he did, he took some black powder and set fire to the holes to close them up."

"He what? Set fire to me?"

"Take a look."

Walter sat up and gingerly removed the bandage from his chest. The hole from the arrow was singed closed as if the skin melted together to seal it up. "Harvey did this?"

"Saved your life," Sweetwater said.

"What about my mail runs?" Walter asked.

"Me and Slick and some of the boys are covering them until you can ride."

Walter nodded and slung his legs over the edge of the bed. "Help me to the table."

Leaning on Sweetwater, Walter walked to the table and sat. He filled the tin cup and drank more water. "By God, I got me a hankering for a Bartlett pear," he said.

"What's that?"

"Sweet, I appreciate all your doings for me, but you are dumb as a pack mule," Walter said. "A Bartlett pear is a— . . . never mind."

The door opened and Harvey walked in with a tin plate full of beans and bacon, with cornbread cakes on the side. He set the plate in front of Walter. "How about a nice glass of rye whiskey to wash this down with?"

Walter nodded as he dug into the food.

Harvey filled three tin cups with rye whiskey and he and Sweetwater sat with Walter at the table.

"What did you do to my arrow wound?" Walter asked as he took a small sip of rye whiskey.

"Cauterized them to seal off the bleeding," Harvey said.

"That's that fancy word, Walter," Sweetwater said.

"I see what you did, what's it mean?"

"I used gunpowder and a match to burn your flesh closed to stop the bleeding," Harvey said. "I didn't have any material for stitching."

"You set fire to my skin?"

"I did," Harvey said.

"I'm grateful I was passed out at the time," Walter said.

"You're a strong boy, Walter," Harvey said. "You'll be back riding the mail in nothing flat."

"Well, at least I didn't lose no teeth," Walter said.

"Just so you know, the Army sent out a squad of men to run down them Paiutes," Harvey said. "They hunted them down and kilt them all twenty miles west of here."

"I'm truly sorry to hear that," Walter said.

"Sorry? Them savages damn near kilt you, Walt."

"Them savages are just defending land they feel is rightfully theirs," Walter said. "I can't fault a man for that. I'd do the same thing."

"Even if they kilt you?" Sweetwater asked.

"They didn't kilt me," Walter said.

"Well, they tried."

"I hate to interrupt this philosophy meeting, but I almost forgot that a letter came for you, Walter," Harvey said. "Slicker brought it in this morning."

"From back east?"

"What's a phil . . . o . . . ?" Sweetwater said.

"Means a deep thinker," Harvey said.

"That's you, Sweet," Walt said. "A deep thinker."

"I'll get your letter, Walt," Harvey said and left the cabin.

"Want some more beans, Walt?" Sweetwater asked.

"No, I'm gonna grab some more sleep."

"What about your letter?"

"I'll read it later."

Fueled by the food and rye whiskey, Walter made it to the

bed under his own steam without the room spinning under his feet. It seemed his head touched the pillow and he was sound asleep.

When Walter opened his eyes next, Sweetwater, Slicker and Harvey were at the table, eating grub. He sat up and as he did so, he let out a loud moan.

"There you are, Walt," Slicker said. "I thought for sure you'd sleep till morning."

Walter slung his legs over the bed and stood up.

"There's plenty of grub left, Walt," Sweetwater said. "Want me to fix you a plate with a cup of rye?"

Walter lumbered to the table. "I surely would."

Sweetwater went to the woodstove and returned with a plate loaded down with fried steak, potatoes, beans, cornbread and gravy. He set the plate in front of Walter and took a chair.

"This Sunday?" Walter said.

Pan-fried steak was usually reserved for Sunday, the lone day of the week all riders rested.

"More like Sunday night," Slicker said.

"And that reminds me," Harvey said and stood up. "I best see to tomorrow's mail. Goodnight, Walter."

"See you in the morning, Harvey," Walter said and cut into his steak.

"How about a shot to wash that down?" Slicker said and opened the bottle of rye on the table. He filled three cups and slid one across the table to Walter.

"Obliged," Walter said.

"You gonna read your letter now?" Sweetwater asked.

"Tell you what, Sweet," Walter said. "Go on and open it and read it to me."

Sweetwater looked at the letter that was still on the table

where Walter left it many hours ago. "Walter, you know I can't.
. . ."

"I been teaching you to read, ain't I?" Walter said.

"From my bible," Sweetwater said. "Not no letter."

"Read it anyway," Walter said. "Slick, you help him."

Sweetwater stared at the sealed envelope for many seconds before he gently reached for it and held it in his hands.

"Unless you're in contact with the spirit world, you have to open it to read what's inside," Walter said.

"I know that," Sweetwater said.

"Use my jackknife," Slicker said as he slid his pocket knife across the table.

Sweetwater picked up the knife, extended the blade and carefully sliced the flap of the envelope open. He set the knife aside and removed the folded page from inside and stared at the words.

"I mean for you to read it aloud," Walter said.

"I'm studying it first, Walter," Sweetwater said.

"Don't study it for too long," Walter said. "I might die from my arrow wound or old age."

"Want me to read it, Walter?" Slicker said.

"No," Walter said. "I want to know I ain't been wasting six months of Sundays teaching him reading."

Sweetwater stared hard at the page. The words were written in pen and ink and the letters were all linked together and different than the letters printed in his good book.

Walter took a sip of rye from his cup. "Anytime, Sweet," he said.

"Don't hurry me, Walter," Sweetwater said. He looked at the letter and started to read the words.

"Dear . . . est, Walter, I hope you are well, and not . . . too tired from all the . . . riding you have to do to pay for my . . . ed . . . ed . . . u . . ."

Slicker looked over Sweetwater's shoulder. "Education, Sweet. Means schooling."

Sweetwater nodded and continued reading. "Your hard work has not gone to waste as I have le . . . learned many new things. I have just read a book called *A Ch . . . Chris . . .*" Sweetwater paused to look at Slicker.

"*A Christmas Carol,*" Slicker said. "Means Christmas story."

Sweetwater nodded. "By Ch . . . arles Dic . . . kens. It is a won . . . der . . . ful story about Christ . . . mas. I also am learn . . . ing a . . . bout the U.S. go . . . gov, oh the government. And how it works. I tell you these things so that you know all the mo . . . ney you send has not been was . . . ted. At school, they me . . . me . . . a . . ."

"Measured," Slicker said.

"Measured me to be five feet and one in . . . ches tall," Sweetwater said. "And have filled out to one hun . . . dred and two pounds. The visi . . . ting doctor said that I am in per . . . fect he . . . alth. I don't mind being here so much as our a . . . a . . . aunt is re . . . eally nice and takes good care of me. New York is really big and sc . . . sc . . ."

"Scary," Slicker said.

"With a lot of people and many tall bu . . . bu . . ."

"Buildings," Slicker said.

"I will write you a . . . again soon and will send you *The Christ . . . mas Carol* for you to read. I love you and miss you very much. Your baby sister, Jo . . . ana."

Sweetwater and Slicker looked at Walter, who hadn't moved a muscle the entire time Sweetwater read the letter.

"Walter?" Slicker said softly.

Walter moved to turn his head.

"Are you okay, Walter?" Slicker said.

Walter picked up his tin cup and finished the rye whiskey in one long gulp, then set the cup down. He picked up the letter, replaced it in the envelope, folded it and tucked it into his pants pocket.

"I'll think I'll sleep for a bit more," Walter said.

CHAPTER SIX

Wyoming 1861

Since the South fired the first shot at Fort Sumter, South Carolina, six months ago, mail and correspondence was dominated by talk of the war. Folks out west writing kin back east for news of family, folks back east writing kin out west with news of the war. Recruitment posters asking young men to join up and fight for the Union, and it was amazing to Walter how many men went east to fight for a cause they had no notion about from territories that weren't even part of the Union. Most men out west, Walter included, had never even seen a Negro and had little understanding of how the government worked, much less the idea behind secession or preservation.

Letters from Joanna came about twice a month. She spoke of the war and how it was changing New York City. She said many people in New York were against the war and President Lincoln. She also said that many people were for the war and believed no man should own another man as property. She wrote that she saw many Negros on the streets and except for the color of their skin, they seemed just like everyone else. She sent him several more books, including another by Dickens.

In early April 1861, Boss called his riders to his station on a Sunday morning.

"Men, even though not a one of you is yet twenty, I consider each one of you to be men," Boss said. "The days of the Pony

Express are numbered to but a few. The telegraph, which can send messages across the country in minutes, will replace us beginning this month. It's nobody's fault here. Each man here has done their job in the service of the country. It's just progress is all, and nothing can stop progress from happening. We will ride one more week, but each man will be paid for the entire month. It has been a privilege knowing each and every one of you and you've all done your country proud."

After the meeting, Walter, Sweetwater and Slicker ate breakfast at a picnic table outside the office.

"Progress, my ass," Walter complained.

"You can't stop it, Walter," Slicker said. "It's just the way things is."

"What's a telegraph, anyway?" Sweetwater asked.

"Don't you never look at the posts sent by the government?" Slicker said.

"No," Sweetwater said. "My job is to carry 'em, not read 'em."

"Like you could, anyway," Walter said.

"The telegraph is them wires you see being strung up on some places along the routes," Slicker said. "They send messages by electricity using a special code. Not long ago, they was asking for people to learn the code and apply for jobs as operators."

"What kind of code?" Sweetwater said. "And what's electricity?"

"The Morse Code," Walter said. "Bunch of dots and dashes used to form letters and words. I read about it in a government poster. And electricity is beyond your comprehension, Sweet. In any event, I can't see how such foolishness will last."

"It will last, Walter," Slicker said. "Progress always lasts once people get a taste of it."

"Maybe so, but I don't have to like it none," Walter said.

"No, but you got to live with it," Slicker said.

"So what do we do now?" Sweetwater asked.

"Well, I been studying on that," Walter said. "As I see it, we got few choices. We can go east and join the war and make eleven dollars a month if we don't get kilt. We can sign on as hands to some of the local ranches starting up around here and make fifteen dollars a month. We can move to towns and work as shopkeepers for less than that. Or, we can become lawmen for hire and earn some real money in reward bounty. Personally, that's what I aim to do on account of my sister needs me to keep sending her money."

"What do you know about being a lawman, Walter?" Slicker asked.

"About as much as you," Walter said. "But, if you read the reward posters we carry, some rewards are as much as two hundred dollars a man."

Slicker and Sweetwater exchanged glances, which didn't go unnoticed by Walter.

"What?" Walter said.

"We been talking, me and Sweet," Slicker said. "About starting up a ranch, maybe in Colorado or Wyoming. The government posts says they is giving away land to settlers."

"I seen those," Walter said. "For farmers, mostly. Homesteaders. Small plots for planting. For cattle, you need grazing land and a lot of it. You need open range, a good cabin and barns, fences and a herd of thousands if you're to make a go of things. You got money for that?"

"Me and Sweet saved a thousand dollars each," Slicker said.

"You'll need many times that," Walter said.

"How much?" Sweetwater said.

"I don't know for sure, but a sight more than you got," Walter said.

"What about you?" Slicker said.

"I sent most of my earnings to my sister, you know that," Walter said. "I reckon I got about three hundred saved. That ain't nearly enough."

"Maybe next week when we're done with our riding duties, we can go to the land office and find out what it will cost to start a spread," Slicker said.

Walter stared at Slicker. "You mean throw in together, the three of us?"

"Three seems quicker than one," Slicker said.

"It couldn't hurt none to find out, Walter," Sweetwater said.

"I guess it couldn't at that," Walter said. "But, however much it is, the quickest way to make that kind of money is as private lawmen. I seen one poster says fifty dollars a man for the capture of Army deserters and from what I understand, there's a bunch of them already."

Slicker and Sweetwater exchanged glances again.

"All right, Walter," Slicker said. "We'll throw in with you as lawmen so long as we use the money for our spread."

"And it don't take too long," Slicker said.

"I'm agreeable to that," Walter said.

"Let's shake on the deal and throw a shot of rye into our coffee," Slicker said.

"I'm agreeable to that, too," Walter said.

CHAPTER SEVEN

New York City 1885

Joanna Beal forced herself to sit up in her large brass bed so she could reach the bottle of laudanum on the nightstand. She removed the cork and took several long swallows, then replaced the cork and bottle and laid her head on the pillow.

Within moments, the powerful mixture of morphine and opium eased the pain in her wretched body enough for her to sit up with little discomfort. Vile-tasting, bitter stuff as it was, it saw her through the roughest of days and nights and allowed her mind to somewhat function as normal.

On those nights when the pain in her back and legs was excruciating, she doubled up on the dose as Doctor Morton suggested. Last night was one of those nights and after four heavy doses, she fell into a drunken, painless sleep.

Fueled by the laudanum, Joanna reached for the pull cord beside the bed and rang it twice. Within a minute, her servant of ten years, a heavyset woman named Alice, entered the bedroom.

"Yes, ma'am?" Alice said somberly.

"Can you fetch my son for me?" Joanna asked.

"Right away, ma'am," Alice said and closed the door behind her.

Moments later, Joanna's son William entered the bedroom. At thirteen, he was thin, frail and sickly. Dressed in proper school clothing—shorts, suit jacket and tie—he tiptoed to the bed.

"Yes, Mother?" William said, barely above a whisper.

"Come closer to me, William," Joanna said.

William approached the bed.

"Will, listen to me carefully," Joanna said. "I haven't much time and there is a great deal to discuss about my death."

William started to sniffle. "I don't want you to die, Mother."

"I don't either, Will," Joanna said. "But the good Lord has made this my time and there is nothing I or the doctors can do about it."

"But why now, Mother?"

"I don't know the answer to that," Joanna said. "I'm sure I'll find out in due time. Right now I need you to stop crying and listen to me carefully. In the drawer of my nightstand is a letter. Reach in and get it for me."

William slid open the drawer and removed the sealed envelope.

"It's addressed to your Uncle Walter, my brother, and I need you to mail it for me without your stepfather knowing," Joanna said. "Can you do that for me?"

"Yes, Mother, but why can't we use the telephone to call him?" William said.

"Oh, William, I'm afraid there aren't any telephones where your uncle lives," Joanna said.

"No telephones?"

"No, now hurry, please."

William nodded, kissed Joanna, turned and scurried out of the room. She immediately grabbed the laudanum bottle and took another hard sip.

Joanna settled back on the pillow, closed her eyes and allowed the laudanum to wash over her like a piece of driftwood on the tide until the pain was gone and she floated away on a snowy cloud.

She knew the letter would not reach her brother in time. She could have posted it sooner, let him know she was ill, but she didn't want her brother to see her die. When she saw him last, she was a healthy, bustling woman of eighteen and full of life and hope for the future. The occasion was her marriage to twenty-one-year-old Wilson Granger, the son of a wealthy New York merchant. They were to honeymoon in Chicago on the lake. They decided to hold the wedding there as well so Walter could attend. Walter made the trip by train for the ceremony.

Joanna was shocked at the change in her older brother. Just nineteen when they saw each other last, Walter was a shy, thin boy, sweet, with an inner softness. The man who showed up at her wedding was a hardened, tough-as-nails sort of twenty-two. He'd grown an inch and filled out to a muscular, imposing frame, but it was in his eyes she saw the changes in him the most. The sweetness and innocence in his eyes was gone, replaced with a hardness that spoke of things that he did that he didn't want to speak about and she didn't want to know about. She heard guests whisper that Walter took up the trade of bounty hunter and had killed several men in the line of duty and wounded many others.

She didn't ask him if it were true, but she saw the answer in his eyes that it was.

However, Walter was still Walter inside and damned if he didn't cry during the ceremony like an old hen.

And he kept his promise and danced with her at her wedding, even if he did step on her feet a time or two.

That was more than twenty years ago.

A lifetime ago.

After the honeymoon, Joanna and Wilson moved into his parents' townhouse on Fifth Avenue, across the street from the newly developed Central Park. They occupied the entire first floor, enough room for a family of eight or ten. They got started immediately on creating a family. She figured that at her age, there was time to raise a dozen or more, but it proved more difficult a task than she imagined. She had several miscarriages. However, after years of trying, she finally conceived and her son was born.

They chose the name William Walter Granger and he was born a sickly child. By the time he was a year old, he'd been in the hospital a half dozen times. She thought, on a few occasions, that she would leave the hospital without her son. But he survived and grew, and even if his health didn't improve, his mind was sharp and intelligent.

When her son was eight, her beloved husband and father-in-law were murdered while riding their carriage across Central Park on their way home from a business meeting. Wretched thieves shot them dead for their wallets and left them there in the road. The city police never found who committed the horrible crime, and the murderers went unpunished.

Having lost her mother-in-law a year earlier to a stroke, Joanna inherited the entire three-story townhouse and the family business on lower Broadway. She met her second husband Jordan Beal, a banker and stockbroker, when William was ten and they married a year later after he proposed to her while they walked in Central Park not far from where Wilson was murdered.

She didn't love Jordan, not the way she loved Wilson, but he was handsome, charming and appeared a fit stepfather for her son, which was her main objective in the marriage. A boy needs a man around growing up. Things were fine for a while. Then Jordan seemed to change and grow cold toward her and William. She grew to mistrust him inside of a year when her bookkeepers informed her that money was missing from the business accounts. He claimed no knowledge of the transactions, but she knew he was stealing from her when she hired a Pinkerton detective to explore the matter and he reported back to her the gambling activities Jordan was engaged in on a regular basis.

Apparently, he was a terrible gambler and his losses were considerable.

Now, with maybe days left before she passed, Joanna prayed to God her letter reached her brother in time to save her son from the life of misery she knew Jordan would inflict upon the boy.

Joanna opened her eyes and looked at the ceiling. "Please, Walter, do what I ask," she said aloud and reached for the laudanum bottle one more time.

CHAPTER EIGHT

Wyoming 1885

The rain and wind were relentless the entire three-day ride to South West City. The rain came down in sheets. The wind blew it at an angle with such force, it stung like bees when it hit you in the face.

The mud-covered streets of South West City were dark and deserted when Walter, Slicker and Sweetwater rode into town, wearing slicker raincoats over their clothing. Not that the slickers did much good against the wind. Wind like that found a way to wet your clothes no matter what you did to keep it out.

The last time Walter had been in South West City, there were maybe a dozen buildings to the entire town. That was in seventy-seven during spring. Shortly after that, some damn fool got it in his head he could find gold coming off the Rocky Mountains where they met the Great Plains, figuring the water would carry gold nuggets and flakes down into the rivers and streams below.

It didn't.

The fool never did find gold, but he did find coal, and lots of it. Within two years, a hub of towns grew up around the mines and made those successful at removing it from the earth very rich men. There was a big demand for coal back east in the big cities, although Walter never had much use for the filthy stuff. Even in a campfire, it billowed foul-smelling black smoke that was useless to cook upon.

As they rode down Main Street toward the livery stables, it

was apparent that South West City had grown quite a bit since they last visited. Forty or fifty buildings took up about ten square acres of land. At least two hundred people now lived inside the town limits, most of them coal miners, although there were some businesses of note usually found in bigger cities.

A large doctor's office took up three buildings on the right, a necessity Walter figured for the health of the miners. A few storefronts down was a dentist office, and across the street from that was an optometrist. Maybe mining for coal ruined a man's teeth and eyesight, along with his lungs.

There was a store with little yellow canary birds in the window, which, Walter heard, the miners took down into the mines with them as a warning device. If the little birds keeled over dead, it was time to leave.

"Grown some," Slicker commented as they neared the livery.

"You'd think a town with this many folks in it would elect a sheriff or a town marshal," Sweetwater said.

"I expect they're too busy working the mines to worry about the law," Walter said.

They reached the closed door of the livery stable.

Walter dismounted and banged on the door. "I know it ain't a fit night for man or beast, but we have three animals need tending to," he shouted.

Next to the wide livery stables, the light from a lantern suddenly illuminated the dark interior. A door slowly slid open and an older man wearing bed clothes held the lantern in his right hand.

"No man should have his animal out on a night like this," the man said. "How many of you, three?"

"I just said that, didn't I?" Walter said.

"I don't hear so good these days, especially with that wind and rain," the man said. "Bring them in."

Walter walked his horse into the stables, while Slicker and

Sweetwater rode in and dismounted once inside.

"We'll be staying the night, so we want them well fed and rested," Walter said. "Is there a hotel in town?"

"Several," the man said. "They all serve food."

"Give them a good brushing." Walter gave the man a ten-dollar piece. "If it ain't enough, we'll settle up in the morning."

"More than enough," the man said.

From his saddle, Walter removed a Winchester 73 rifle, as did Sweetwater. Slicker preferred the heavier Henry rifle and removed it from his saddle.

They stepped out into the rain, then up onto the wood plank sidewalk where an overhanging roof provided some shelter.

"We'll do this as usual," Walter said.

"You sure he's in the Metropole Saloon?" Sweetwater said.

"That's what the marshal over in Denver said," Walter said. "Dealing cards for the house."

"Let me see that bill again so I know we don't make no mistake and grab the wrong man," Sweetwater said.

"For Christ sake, Sweet," Slicker said. "You seen it ten times already."

"Show him the bill before he gets started again," Walter said.

Slicker dug the folded bill from an inside pocket and gave it to Sweetwater. The bill was a wanted poster with a black and white photograph of Silver McFee, whereas ten years ago, it would have been a hand-drawn sketch. The bill read, WANTED: Silver McFee for murder. $2500 reward. Dead or alive.

"Satisfied?" Slicker asked.

Sweetwater nodded.

"You'd never know we'd been doing this more than twenty years the way you carry on like an old hen," Slicker said.

"Well, I'm ready," Sweetwater said.

"Then let's quit talking about it and go do it," Walter said.

Shoulder-to-shoulder, they walked several blocks west to the center of town where the Metropole Saloon dominated the block. It was as wide and as lavish as any saloon in Denver, except for maybe the Gentlemen's Club, which was actually a high-class brothel for Denver's elite businessmen.

They stood outside for a moment and peered through the double swinging doors. Six large card tables were full of players. Four games tables, including craps and the wheel, were also crowded. The bar was polished redwood and drinkers were lined up. A piano player played a tune in the corner. Saloon girls, scantily dressed, smiled, served drinks and for the right price, serviced you on the second floor by way of the stairs beside the piano player.

Walter flipped open his slicker to reveal the deputy marshal's badge pinned to his shirt. Slicker and Sweetwater did the same. Walter went in first, closely followed by Slicker and Sweetwater.

With practiced precision, Walter, Slicker and Sweetwater cocked the levers of the rifles in unison. It got immediate attention. The word on the Metropole was that firearms weren't allowed inside and even though sidearms weren't visible, Walter had little doubt every man was packing at minimum a .32-caliber belly gun.

"I want nobody in this room to move," Walter said loudly. "Any man moves and I'll take that as a sign he's reaching for a gun and I will shoot you down where you sit or stand. Am I clear?"

Every eye was on Walter.

"As you can see by these badges on our shirts, we are here on official business," Walter said. "So any man interferes in our business will be dealt with directly and harshly."

Walter swung his Winchester around until the barrel settled on Silver McFee.

"A U.S. senator was shot and kilt by a murderous card cheat down in Texas," Walter said. "After the senator befriended him, this man shot him and stole fifty dollars and a gold watch given to him by his family."

The saloon was suddenly abuzz with chatter.

"Shut up, all a ya!" Walter shouted. "We have an official warrant to bring in Silver McFee, who is seated right there at the end of my Winchester."

There was a sudden noise and Walter turned to see the bartender reaching behind the bar for something.

"Freeze right there, mister," Walter said. "Slick, go see what fancy pants there is grabbing for. If it ain't a free beer for me, bust him open."

Slicker walked to the bar and jabbed the bartender with his massive Henry rifle. "Stand back," he said.

The bartender stepped back until he was against the long row of whiskey bottles. Slicker reached over the bar with his left hand and came up with a double-barrel shotgun, cocked. He opened the breech, removed the two shells, closed the breech and smashed the heavy stock into the bartender's nose.

"You ain't none too smart, are you?" Slicker said as the bartender crashed into the row of bottles and fell to the floor, taking a few bottles with him.

"Anybody else want to play Custer?" Walter said.

A nervous-looking man with a bald head and walrus mustache sitting at McFee's table cleared his throat.

"You?" Walter said. "You got something to say?"

The man shook his head no.

"All right, McFee, stand up real slow," Walter said.

McFee didn't move. "I ain't never been to Texas, mister," he said. "You got the wrong man."

"I told you to stand up," Walter said. "I won't be telling you again."

Slowly, McFee got to his feet.

"Hands on the table where I can see them," Walter said.

McFee started to put his hands on the table, and then reached inside his jacket for a hidden .32 revolver.

Walter cracked him across the nose with the Winchester and McFee fell to the floor with a violent thud, losing the .32 revolver.

"Not smart," Walter said. "Get up."

With blood running down his nose, McFee looked up at Walter.

"You heard me," Walter said.

Slowly, McFee rose to his feet.

"Will you go quiet?" Walter said.

McFee nodded his head.

"Slick, break out them irons," Walter said.

From inside his slicker, Slick produced a set of heavy handcuffs. As he approached him, McFee withdrew a long knife from inside his jacket.

Walter lunged forward and smacked McFee in the jaw with the Winchester. McFee went down and this time he was out cold.

"That was a decision not based upon intelligence," Walter said. He nodded to Slicker, who bent down to cuff McFee.

"My intention is not cruelty, but your town is better off without this murderous scum in it," Walter said.

The man with the walrus moustache finally worked up the courage to speak. He looked at Walter, cleared his throat and said, "We see your badges and you lay claim to a warrant, but I know I would feel a great deal better about you removing a man this way if you could provide a little more proof to your claim."

"You would, would you," Walter said. "Slick, check his pockets."

Slicker felt through McFee's pockets and stood up holding a gold watch. He tossed it to Walter.

"You like to talk," Walter said and tossed the watch to the

man with the walrus moustache. "Read it."

Nervously, the man opened the cover of the watch. "To Senator John Mitchell, from his loving family."

"Happy now?" Walter said.

The man with the walrus moustache nodded and tossed the watch back to Walter.

"You got anything that resembles a jail in this town?" Walter asked.

"Behind the dentist's office is a holding cell," the man with the walrus moustache said. "The dentist has the key."

"Is he here?"

"That would be me," the man with the walrus moustache said. "I'm the dentist."

"Lead the way," Walter said. "We'll be there as soon as we awaken sleeping beauty there."

"Are you really a dentist?" Sweetwater said after McFee was safely locked away in the small cell connected to the dentist's office by a door and hallway.

"Look around you, sir," the dentist said. "What do you see?"

Sweetwater, Walter and Slicker looked around the office. There were two reclining chairs with trays laid out with picks and tools. There were cabinets filled with drugs and whatnots and shelves of fake teeth.

"I got me a tooth bothering me," Sweetwater said. "I wonder if you could have a look-see at it."

"It's after ten at night," the dentist said.

"I'd be obliged," Sweetwater said. "It's really acting up."

The dentist sighed. "Have a seat."

"When you get through with your dentistering, me and Slick will be having something to eat at the hotel there across the street," Walter said.

Sweetwater sat in a chair. "This ain't gonna hurt, will it?" he said.

"I hope so," the dentist said.

CHAPTER NINE

Walter and Slicker met for breakfast at the hotel dining room the following morning. They ordered steak and eggs, with a pot of coffee, biscuits and jam.

"See Sweet this morning?" Walter asked.

"There he is now," Slicker said.

Sweetwater came down the stairs and took the vacant seat at the table.

"The doc fix you up last night?" Walter asked.

Sweetwater nodded. "Said I had me a cavity in my tooth," he said. "He rubbed something on my gums and scraped away at it with the pick until he said it was clean. Then he filled it with gold."

"What?" Slicker said. "Gold?"

Sweetwater opened his mouth to show the gold filling. Walter and Slicker leaned in close for a look.

"I'll be damned," Slicker said. "That is gold."

"He said my tooth was worth more than my whole head," Sweetwater said.

"I believe him. Close your mouth before you catch flies and order some breakfast," Walter said. "We have to ride to Rock Springs and send a wire to the marshal back home and the senator's family that McFee will be on the train out of Rock Springs to Texas."

"If they had a telephone, we could call them," Slicker said.

Sweetwater grinned.

"Don't get me started on no telephones," Walter said.

"It's progress, Walt," Slicker said. "You can't stop it none."

"I don't plan to stop it, just ignore it. Go ahead and order your breakfast, Sweet," Walter said. "I have some figuring to do."

Sweetwater flagged a waitress while Walter dug out his small ledger book and pencil. By the time Sweetwater was finished eating, Walter had the calculations in order.

"With the senator's reward money thrown in the pot, we got thirty-two thousand dollars in that Lincoln Bank," Walter said. "Another eight thousand and we have our ranch, lock, stock and barrel, cattle included."

Slicker and Sweetwater exchanged glances.

"What?" Walter said. "I know when you two hens start looking at each other it means you got something to say, so say it."

"Eight thousand dollars means working another year," Slicker said.

"It does," Walter said. "What of it?"

"It's my opinion that we have enough to get started right now," Slicker said. "Our spread don't have to be the biggest in the state, you know."

Walter looked at Sweetwater. "How about you?"

"I didn't say nothing," Sweetwater said.

"I know you didn't," Walter said. "I'm asking if you have something to contribute to the conversation."

"I think I agree with Slick," Sweetwater said.

"You think?" Walter said. "Think ain't an opinion, you mush head."

"Now, Walt, there ain't no reason to get in one of your moods," Slicker said. "We ain't kids no more and we think it's time we did what we set out to do before we're in rocking chairs."

"I know we ain't kids," Walter said. "But, we ain't exactly old men, neither."

"I think we need to get our ranch before we're too old to do much but sit on the porch and drink whiskey," Slicker said. "Both me and Sweet feel the same way."

"Worried about your old age, are you?" Walter said.

"Oh, to hell with old age," Slicker said. "All I'm saying is I'd rather spend what good years I got left building our ranch than chasing some no-good outlaws."

Walter looked at Sweetwater. "You agree with him?"

"I kind of like what Slick said, Walt," Sweetwater said.

"Which part, the rocking chair or the ranch?" Walter said.

"All of it," Sweetwater said.

"It's time, Walter," Slicker said. "I got twenty good years left in me, and I don't want to waste them on any more Silver Mc-Fees."

Walter sat back in his chair and thought for a moment. "Maybe you're right," he said. "When we get home and collect our money, we can start out for Lincoln and talk to them bankers. Before winter sets in, maybe we can pick up some extra reward money on some local boys along the way for a cushion."

"Agreed," Slicker said.

"Me, too," Sweetwater said.

Walter pulled out his tobacco pouch and rolling paper and started to roll a cigarette.

"Hey, Walter?" Slicker said. "I heard they getting a talking machine at the Denver Fair this fall."

"What's that?" Sweetwater said.

"They say you talk into the little box and it talks back to you whatever you said," Slicker said. "I hear it was invented by Mr. Thomas Edison himself."

"What useful purpose is there in talking to a box that repeats back your own words to you?" Walter said.

"You said the same thing about the telephone and now look,

they just about everywhere," Slicker said.

"Not everywhere," Walter said. "Not yet."

"You know what your problem is, Walt," Slicker said. "You don't like the idea of progress."

Walter glared at Slicker. "To hell with the both of you hens," he said, and stood up and stormed away.

Sweetwater cracked up laughing. "One of these days, you will push him too far and I'll have to pull him off you."

"I know it," Slicker grinned.

Sweetwater finished his coffee, and then said, "Hey, Slick, who's Thomas Edison?"

CHAPTER TEN

Colorado Springs was quickly becoming the hub of the western states. It was sprawling, loud and filled with people. Some ten thousand people at last count, according to the newspaper reports, Walter remembered as they rode down Main Street. Soon it would rival Denver in its size and modern living conditions.

That was too many people in one place to suit Walter. Slicker was right, of course, it was time to buy their ranch and get out of the city. It seemed that every time they returned from a trip, ten new buildings had sprung up because of the railroad station. Shops mostly, places where folks could buy their whatnots from back east. Telegraph poles were everywhere on Main Street, and Walter knew it wouldn't be too long before those poles carried the lines necessary for the telephone. Within five years, he imagined. Maybe less. Who knew what else they would come up with back east and bring out west that took up living space and fresh air and water?

A carriage powered by a single horse passed them on Main Street. That was another thing that annoyed Walter about big towns; nobody seemed to ride a horse anymore, preferring carriages and wagons to the saddle.

On Ridge Street, they turned right and rode to the end of the block to the large livery stables where they dismounted.

"Bring my saddlebags to the house," Walter said. "I'm going to see the marshal and make sure our reward money is on the way to the bank in Lincoln."

"You done checked on it twice, Walt," Slicker said.

"I know, but before we ride there, I want to be sure it got there ahead of us," Walter said. "Besides, I want to see if there's some new rewards posted we can pick up on the trip. I'll see you back at the house."

Walter walked back to Main Street where he removed his gun belt and slung the heavy Peacemaker over his shoulder. Even though the special deputy marshal's badge gave him the right to carry a sidearm out in the open in a town where it was forbidden by a half dozen codes, he knew the sight of such a massive weapon upset the delicate stomachs of some shopkeepers and their prissy womenfolk customers.

At the end of the block, Walter paused to look behind him to make sure he wasn't seen by anybody he knew and then he turned and entered the optometrist shop just around the corner.

The optometrist, Doctor Baker, a smallish man of about fifty, came out from a back room and approached Walter as he hung the gun belt on a hat rack.

"Hi, Doc," Walter said. "My name is . . ."

"Walter Burke, yes I know," Baker said. "You and your partners are somewhat famous men in town. What can I help you with?"

"It's my eyes, Doc," Walter said. "I'm having a slight problem."

"Oh? What kind of a slight problem?"

"Well, I see just fine when I'm looking at things," Walter said. "But, lately, when I'm reading or writing, things get a bit fuzzy up close."

Baker smiled and said, "You're over forty, aren't you, Mr. Burke?"

"Forty-four next birthday," Walter said. "Why?"

"At a certain age, our eyes fail to adjust to dim light or smaller print," Baker said. "It happens to almost everyone and is perfectly normal. Let's check your vision. Would you stand at that yellow line on the floor there?"

Walter moved to the painted yellow line on the wood floor.

"See that chart on the wall?" Baker said. "Cover your left eye and read it for me to the smallest line possible."

Walter covered his left eye and read the chart.

"Now the other eye," Baker said.

Walter covered his right eye and read the chart.

"You see just fine, Mr. Burke," Baker said. "You didn't miss one letter. Sit in the chair and I'll check for cataracts."

Walter took the chair. "What's that?"

"Something I doubt you have, Mr. Burke."

Using a candle inside a specially designed lantern that threw a beam of light, Baker carefully examined Walter's eyes.

"Your eyes are fine, Mr. Burke. Healthy as can be. Let's try some reading spectacles," Baker said.

Baker removed a pair of spectacles from inside a glass counter and gave them to Walter. "Put these on and read this fine newspaper print," Baker said.

Walter slipped the spectacles on and took the newspaper from Baker. "It's clear as day, Doc," Walter said. "Even the tiny print on top."

"I think you'll find in very bright light, such as direct sunlight, you won't need the spectacles, but indoors where it's dimmer, you will," Baker said. "I suggest you have an eye exam every year to check your vision, because one day, you'll find you'll need a prescription set of glasses for reading."

"I'll do that," Walter said.

"Oh, one more thing," Baker said. "Don't use them for anything but reading. If you forget and leave them on, it can make you dizzy."

"Thanks, Doc," Walter said. "What do I owe you?"

"Seven dollars," Baker said. "I'll throw in the carrying case for free."

With the spectacles tucked away in his shirt pocket, Walter slung his gun belt over his shoulder and walked to the center of town to the federal marshal's office. Marshal Tom Landon was a fine man and a good marshal. He had offices in a dozen towns inside the state. His responsibilities were federal and he played no part in enforcing the local laws inside the limits of Colorado Springs unless called upon to assist the sheriff and his men. Landon had a dozen deputy marshals for the state and it wasn't nearly enough to get the job done.

Landon was doing paperwork behind his wood desk when Walter entered the marshal's office. Landon had a cup of coffee on the desk and was smoking a hand-rolled cigarette.

"How's things, Tom?" Walter said. "Spare a cup of coffee?"

"Behind you on the woodstove," Landon said.

Walter filled a tin cup with hot coffee and took a chair opposite the desk. "You get my wire?"

"I did," Langston said. "And the senator's family is grateful that you didn't kill McFee. They aim to have him tried and hanged. They said you will receive an additional five hundred dollars for your troubles and for returning the gold watch."

"That's good to know," Walter said. He pulled out his tobacco pouch and paper and rolled a cigarette. "That puts us just that much closer to our ranch."

"Why don't you let me swear you three in full time?" Landon said. "I could sure use three good men for a few years. I find I'm spending more of my time in Denver and I could use the help here."

"Thanks for the offer, Tom," Walter said. "But them two hens I'm married to is hell bent on getting our ranch before the snow falls. We'll be on our way to Lincoln in the next few days to see the bankers."

"Might be some wanted posters coming in the afternoon mail if you're interested in picking up some cash on the way back," Landon said.

"I'm going for a shave and a Chinese bath," Walter said. "If you get any, that's where I'll be."

"Maybe we can have supper later and a drink?" Landon said.

Walter finished his smoke and coffee and stood up. "Be nice to have an intelligent conversation for a change," he said.

CHAPTER ELEVEN

The Ling family ran one of several bathhouses in town. Walter preferred theirs to the others because they did your laundry as well and also served excellent tea while you took your bath.

Walter stripped down to his long underwear to shave carefully in one of the mirrors in the bathhouse while Mrs. Ling filled one of a dozen brass tubs with hot water and salts. Mr. Ling never filled the tubs or did laundry. That was women's work. Truth was, in the years Walter had been frequenting Ling's, he had no idea what Mr. Ling did except greet customers at the door and collect money. Maybe that was enough.

"Bath ready," Mrs. Ling said in her thick accent.

"Go on, now," Walter said. "I'll ring the bell for more hot water and salt when I need it."

"You have laundry?" Mrs. Ling said.

"Not with me," Walter said. "I'll drop it off later."

Mrs. Ling nodded, bowed slightly and left the main room of the bathhouse. Walter finished scraping the stubble from his face, then went to the tub, removed his long underwear and slowly submerged himself in the hot water.

Once fully submerged, Walter splashed hot, salted water on his face to ease the sting of the after-shave burn. The salt stung for a moment, then as he splashed more water on his face, his skin felt cooler.

After a few minutes, Walter's entire body relaxed and the weariness of the trail left his muscles and bones. Beside the tub was a small table that held a bar of soap, a bottle of salts and a small brass bell. He used the soap to scrub his body and wash his hair, then rang the bell a few times for Mrs. Ling.

She appeared from the front room almost immediately.

"A few buckets of hot water would do nicely," Walter said.

Mrs. Ling nodded, returned to the front room and moments later carried in two buckets of hot water directly to the tub. Mrs. Ling wasn't shy around her male customers. Walter figured she'd seen more men's privates than all the bottles of whiskey combined in all the saloons in Denver.

"Rinse hair?" Mrs. Ling said in her accent.

"Rinse hair," Walter said.

Walter bowed his head to allow Mrs. Ling to pour hot water over his hair to rinse out the soap, then she poured the remaining water over his back.

"Thank you kindly, Mrs. Ling," Walter said.

"Ring when finished," Mrs. Ling said and returned to the front room.

Walter lowered his head to the rim of the tub and closed his eyes. A few seconds later, footsteps caused him to open his eyes and he was surprised to see Marshal Landon entering the room.

"Here for a bath or to give me new wanted posters?" Walter said.

"Neither," Landon said. "Got two pieces of mail for you that came addressed to my office in care of you. I almost forgot about them. They're from back east."

"Set them there beside the bell," Walter said. "I'll read them later."

Landon nodded and set the two envelopes on the table. "See you later for that drink," he said.

"You bet."

After Landon left, Walter stayed in the tub until the water started to cool. He reached for the bell and rang it twice. Mrs.

Ling came in with fresh towels and set them on the table beside the tub.

"I think I'll have a cup of your tea out back," Walter said.

"Noodles or cookie?" Mrs. Ling said.

"Not today," Walter said. "I don't want to ruin my appetite for supper."

Mrs. Ling nodded and left the room.

After dressing, Walter carried the two letters with him to the front room where Mrs. Ling led him through a door that opened up to a backyard garden where several tables were located. She guided him to a table in the shade of a massive tree.

"I bring tea," Mrs. Ling said and returned inside.

Walter rolled a smoke while Mrs. Ling went for the tea. She returned with a pot and one of her little cups and set it on the table.

"You want cookie?" she said.

"I believe the tea will suit me just fine for now," Walter said and tossed the spent cigarette under his boot.

Mrs. Ling bowed and went inside. Walter filled the cup with tea and took a sip. Usually, he steered away from tea, but the Chinese tea Mrs. Ling served was different than other teas. He took another sip, then picked up one of the two envelopes. The letters were fuzzy in the shaded light and he reached inside his jacket for the spectacles. Before putting them on, Walter looked around to see if anyone was watching. No one was and he perched the spectacles on his nose.

The first letter was a Western Union Telegram from a lawyer back east named Roland Sands. The content of the telegram was to inform Walter that his sister Joanna Beal passed away in her sleep three nights ago. Sands informed Walter that his presence was required in New York for the reading of Joanna's last will and testament by an attorney selected by Joanna to prepare her will.

Walter sat in shock for many long minutes.

The other letter was addressed to him from Joanna and written in her familiar handwriting.

Walter picked up the letter and carefully tore open the envelope. Before he removed the letter from the envelope he rolled a fresh cigarette and struck a match.

CHAPTER TWELVE

Slicker and Sweetwater were just sitting down to a nice supper at the restaurant across the street from their boardinghouse when Walter walked in looking paler than a ghost and sick to his stomach.

Walter took a seat at the table and immediately waved a waiter over for a glass of rye whiskey.

"What is it, Walt?" Slicker said. "You look like a man with a case of indigestion."

The waiter arrived with the rye. Walter picked up the glass and swallowed half in one long gulp.

"Jeeze, Walt," Sweetwater said. "Ain't like you to drink like that on an empty stomach."

"I just received word from back east that my . . . that Joanna has passed away," Walter said.

Slicker and Sweetwater stared at Walter, their faces registering their shock.

"Six months she was dying of consumption and never wrote me a word about it," Walter said. "She went in her sleep three days before the telegram arrived at the marshal's office."

"I . . . I don't know what to say, Walt," Slicker said.

"Ain't nothing to say," Walter said. "It happened and that's all there is to it."

"What are you going to do?" Sweetwater said.

"Joanna has made a last request of me," Walter said. "About her son."

71

"Little William?" Slicker said.

"The boy is thirteen now," Walter said. "I expect he ain't so little no more. And for some reason, she wants me to go to New York and take the boy by train to San Francisco to live with the boy's aunt and uncle from Joanna's first marriage. The boy is to attend some fancy school there, according to her letter."

"Go to New York?" Sweetwater said.

Walter looked at Sweetwater and Slicker. "What?"

"Nothing, Walt," Slicker said. "We can't see you in New York is all."

"And what would you know about New York?" Walter said.

"I know enough that you won't fit in with them dudes looking like some broke cowhand off the range," Slicker said.

"What are you saying?" Walter said.

"When are you planning to go?" Slicker said.

"Tomorrow on the first train east."

"I suggest you visit the men's store on Main Street and pick out the best eastern dude clothes they got," Slicker said. "They got racks of the stuff for all the dandies in town now."

"That ain't a bad idea," Walter said.

"I believe they open at eight in the morning," Slicker said.

"While I'm gone, which I believe will be the better part of a month, why don't you two ride over to Lincoln and meet with the bankers about finding us a spread," Walter said. "You can wire me in New York with the results. When I'm done delivering the boy we can meet up at the old line shack and make our plans."

"Okay, Walter," Slicker said. "We'll do just that."

"If I can say a word without getting sloppy, I'd like to drink a toast to my sister," Walter said.

Slicker and Sweetwater each had a glass of rye and the three of them clinked the glasses together.

"A man never had a finer sister," Walter said, and downed his rye. "And now if you will excuse me, I'll be going over to my room."

Walter left the table.

"You figure he's all right?" Sweetwater said.

"I figure Walter is the kind of man who won't be seen in public with a tear in his eye," Slicker said.

"Yeah," Sweetwater agreed.

CHAPTER THIRTEEN

Wearing a very fashionable black frock coat with matching trousers and a white shirt with proper tie, Walter perched the bola hat on his head as he exited the men's haberdashery store on Main Street.

Slicker and Sweetwater waited for Walter on the wood sidewalk. A large satchel rested between them. Slicker handed Walter his holster and Peacemaker.

"You look like the preacher man who read to us from the bible back on the river," Sweetwater said.

Walter slung the heavy holster around his waist and settled the frock coat over it. "Was he packing a .45?" he said.

"Don't believe he was," Sweetwater said.

"Train going east leaves at ten thirty," Slicker said.

Walter reached into the watch pocket for the new watch and chain he purchased with the suit. "According to my new watch, that is in exactly twenty-one minutes."

Slicker picked up Walter's satchel. "We'll see you off."

They walked to the end of Main Street where the railroad depot was located. Walter purchased a one-way ticket to New York City on a sleeper car. The train was already in the depot and ready to go as soon as it finished taking on coal and water.

"I'll wire you in Lincoln from New York and let you know what my immediate plans are," Walter said.

"We'll stay at the usual Lincoln Hotel across from the bank," Slicker said. "I understand the banks will be getting telephones right soon so they can keep in touch with the stock market. You might call the bank and leave word."

"I doubt they got telephones so soon in Lincoln," Walter said.

"What's a stock market?" Sweetwater said.

"Something beyond your comprehension," Walter said. "Goodbye, boys, I'll see you in a month or so."

"I put some reading material in your bag I bought at the drugstore," Slicker said.

"Appreciate it," Walter said and stepped aboard the waiting train.

Walter selected a comfortable window seat in a middle car that wasn't too crowded. After many minutes of listening to the engine power up to full steam, the train made a sudden jerk forward and they were in motion. For the first few miles, he watched the scenery roll by from the window, but it all looked the same and he grew bored with it and opened his satchel to see what Slicker put in there.

There was a copy of the *Denver Post* wrapped around a thick book titled *Tour Guide to New York City.*

Walter selected the book, opened it and then set it back in favor of the newspaper. He glanced at the headlines, then looked around to see if anyone else in the car was watching him. They were not and he removed the spectacles from an inside pocket of the frock coat and slipped them on his nose.

After reading every word in the newspaper, Walter took a nap in his seat. When he awoke, he was famished and walked several cars back to the dining car, carrying the guide book with him. He found a vacant table, but the car filled up quickly. He ordered a steak and a sarsaparilla, then put on the spectacles and opened the book.

It wasn't long before every table in the car was full and a young, pretty woman stood over Walter and cleared her throat.

"I do apologize, sir, but there are no available tables," she said. "May I infringe on your hospitality and ask to share yours?"

Walter closed the book and looked at the woman. "Are you any good at conversation?" he said.

"I believe so."

"Then please sit," Walter said and removed the spectacles.

"My name is Sally Winston," she said as she took the chair opposite Walter.

"Walter Burke," Walter said. "Are you traveling alone, a young woman such as yourself?"

Sally smiled. "I travel alone all the time, Mr. Burke. My family considers it part of my education."

"I see," Walter said.

Sally glanced at the tour book. "Are you going to New York City, Mr. Burke?"

Walter removed the spectacles and set them on the table. "Yes, I am."

"It's a wonderful city," Sally said. "I've been there many times."

"This will be my first time east of Missouri since the war," Walter said. "I never did make it north of Virginia."

"My family is from Pittsburg," Sally said. "They are in the steel business. It's quite dull and I travel to New York every opportunity I get."

"Mind if I ask why?"

"Why, for the adventure, of course," Sally said. "And for the education of visiting the museums and libraries."

Walter tapped the tour book with a finger. "Says in here they got a park on the island of Manhattan where you can rent a horse for fun. Why would you do that?"

"Yes, Central Park," Sally said. "And because most people ride carriages, walk or take the electric rail across town."

"So what you're saying is you ride a horse for fun and not to get from one place to another?" Walter said.

"That's one way to look at it," Sally said.

"The book says they got buildings a hundred or more feet tall with outhouses built right in them," Walter said.

Sally giggled.

"I didn't mean to offend," Walter said.

"You didn't."

The waiter came by and took Sally's order.

"If I may ask, Mr. Burke, what is so obvious a cowboy going to New York for?" Sally said. "Even with that frock coat, it is obvious you are no man of the east."

"It seemed like a good time to visit my sister's boy," Walter said. "They live in New York, you see."

"I see," Sally said. "If I may make a suggestion, Mr. Burke. That Colt under your frock coat is forbidden in New York City. Even some of the police only carry sticks and whistles."

"I know about the sticks," Walter said. "But, of what use is a whistle?"

Sally grinned. "I am traveling home to Pittsburg, Mr. Burke. We will have many days to discuss the differences between the east and west."

Later that evening, when Walter was in his berth inside his private sleeping car, he put on the spectacles and read some more in the tour book. He read a story about the elevated train they were constructing that would travel from someplace called The Bronx, clear through Manhattan and all the way to someplace else called Brooklyn, powered only by electricity. The tracks would be as high as forty feet or more above the sidewalk.

Walter removed the spectacles and closed the book.

"I swear," he said to himself.

Days later, as the train neared Pittsburg, Walter and Sally took a final breakfast together in the dining car.

"I will miss our daily conversations, Mr. Burke," Sally said.

"Hearing about your exploits with your partners, I feel like part of your family."

"Maybe when you marry that man you told me about and settle down, you can visit me on our ranch," Walter said.

"Oh, Larry," Sally said as she rolled her eyes.

"That's his name, isn't it?" Walter said. "And from what you told me, he sounds like a right smart fellow."

"And as dull as yesterday's bathwater," Sally said. "I'm only marrying him because both families want it. Larry's family is in steel also, you see. I do believe the Carnegies want to rule the world one day."

"Maybe it might seem dull to you now, but one day you'll appreciate the comforts of a fine home and money," Walter said.

"I believe that to be true," Sally said with sadness in her voice.

The train rolled to a slow stop as it entered the station at Pittsburg.

"I'm afraid this is where I get off, Mr. Burke," Sally said.

"I'll see you out," Walter said.

Walter took Sally's arm and escorted her to the exit car where they paused before she stepped out onto the platform.

"Do you see that man waiting there by the carriage?" Sally said.

"The bespectacled one in the fine suit?" Walter said.

"That's Larry."

"I see why you travel so much," Walter said.

"Remember the things I told you about New York," Sally said.

"I will remember," Walter said.

Sally looked at Walter, and then she broke out into a wide smile. "I will miss you, Mr. Burke," she said and kissed him on the cheek.

Walter watched as Sally walked down to Larry and gave him

a similar kiss on the cheek. As Larry helped her into the carriage, Sally turned, smiled at Walter and waved goodbye.

Twenty-four hours later, Walter sat in stunned silence in his window seat as the train rolled into Manhattan and he got his first look at New York City.

CHAPTER FOURTEEN

The noise alone was enough to make a man plug his ears with cotton. Steam from the trains inside the terminal clogged the air as a thousand people scurried to catch their trains. A giant clock was centered inside the building and below it was a large blackboard with departing and arrival times written on it in chalk. With no idea where he was or where to go next, Walter spotted a booth marked INFORMATION and he walked to it and looked at the man behind the glass.

"Maybe you can help me, sir," Walter said. "I need directions to my destination on the street."

"I don't give information on the streets," the man behind the glass said. "Look for a policeman, he can tell you."

Walter walked away from the booth and as luck would have it, he spotted a man wearing the blue uniform of a policeman. He carried a long stick and wore a brass whistle around his neck. He was armed with a small .32 revolver that wouldn't stop a coyote pup, much less a man.

"Excuse me, but I was wondering if you might give me directions?" Walter said.

The policeman gave Walter a quick onceover. "Have you an address?"

Walter removed Joanna's letter from inside his coat and showed it to the policeman. "Upstairs to the street," he said.

"Upstairs?" Walter said.

"You are underground, sir," the policeman said. "Go upstairs

80

and turn right, then walk two blocks to Fifth Avenue. Turn north and travel to 66th Street and it's right opposite the park."

Walter returned the letter to his pocket. "Appreciate it."

"Don't mention it," the policeman said and rushed away, blowing his whistle at something or another.

Walter found the stairs to the street and followed a crowd up them to a street marked 43rd Street. He was immediately overwhelmed by the sights, sounds and smells of the country's largest metropolis that dwarfed even San Francisco.

Every building in front of him seemed a hundred feet tall. The wide, paved street was clogged with horse-drawn carriages moving in both directions. The sidewalk made of cement was filled with a thousand folks and each one of them seemed in one big hurry to get wherever they were going.

Walter looked at the street sign and figured that if he started at 43rd Street, he would have to walk twenty-three of these blocks to reach 66th Street. He remembered what Sally told him about walking in New York. She said numbered streets went north and south and streets ending with Avenue went east and west. He moved with the crowd and started walking north.

Each block seemed to bring larger, taller buildings, more people and more carriages in the street. Where the hell were they all going? he wondered as he crossed 50th Street along Fifth Avenue. He didn't see houses where people could live in and the necessary shops where they could work in to support so large a population.

At an intersection, he stopped to watch a man sweeping horse manure with a broom, while another man shoveled it into a horse-drawn wagon. It seemed to him a job of futility as the horse pulling the wagon made his own contribution.

He continued on and passed something that stopped him dead in his tracks. It was the biggest church he'd ever seen, a massive, ornate structure with a towering peak that dwarfed its surrounding buildings. Bigger even than the churches he'd seen in Chicago back in seventy-one when they chased an outlaw who was hiding out in the Chicago stockyards before they closed them.

Walter climbed the steps and opened the door and peered inside. Massive stained-glass windows glowed in the sunlight. A giant altar adorned with gold centered on an elevated platform. Statues of every kind hung from the walls. It was staggering what man could create when he put his mind to it. He tipped his hat to a woman exiting the church.

"Would you know the name of this church, ma'am?" Walter said.

"Yes, sir," she said. "Saint Patrick's Cathedral."

"Thank you. I will remember that."

Walter climbed down the stairs to the sidewalk where a man wearing a frock coat similar to his tipped his hat and smiled at Walter. "You have the look of a man in need of a carriage," he said.

"What?" Walter said.

"You do know what a carriage is, sir?" the man said.

Walter looked past the man at the carriage and horse beside him. "I saw my first carriage before you were born," Walter said. "The question is, why would I need one now?"

"My job, sir, is to take people who appear to be lost where they want to go," the man said. "You appear to be lost."

"I'm that obvious?" Walter said.

"Like heat on a fire, sir."

"In that case, can you take me to my sister's place of residence?" Walter asked. "All I have is the address."

"Climb aboard, sir," the man said. "I'll do my best to find it for you."

The man knew exactly where he was going and about three-quarters of a mile later, they arrived at the correct address. The ride was interesting enough. The buildings were large and imposing to behold, but between such buildings were many smaller homes sprinkled in that the man said were called townhouses. Turned out that Joanna had lived in such a townhouse.

Walter paid the man one dollar for the ride and another for his good company. He held the carriage and stood on the sidewalk, holding his satchel. He checked the address of the townhouse against the address on the envelope to be sure. The house itself was four stories tall, with an ornate doorway and a large fenced-in garden to its left. A woman was tending flowers in the garden.

Walter approached the woman. "Good morning to you, miss," he said.

The woman stood up and looked at Walter. "Deliveries are around back at the servant's door. Ring the bell."

"Deliveries?" Walter said. "The only thing I'm delivering is myself. My name is Walter Burke and my sister Joanna lived here with her husband and son. She wrote me and I've traveled a long way to get here."

The woman came around and exited the garden and stood before Walter. "I see the resemblance," she said. "I apologize, sir. My name is Alice and I served your sister for many years."

"Nice to know you, Alice," Walter said. "Can you tell me which rooms are hers?"

"Why, all of them, sir," Alice said, somewhat surprised at Walter's question. "The entire house was your sister's property."

Walter looked up at the building, its windows and elaborate balcony on the fourth floor. "All of it?" he said.

"Yes, sir," Alice said. "Come inside. I'll get Mr. Duffy for you right away."

Alice opened the frosted glass front door and escorted Walter into a vast parlor that was furnished in expensive cherry wood furniture.

"Mr. Duffy won't be but a moment, sir," Alice said and left the parlor.

Walter barely had time to inspect the furniture before Mr. Duffy, a man of about sixty and dressed in a butler's suit, entered the parlor. "Mr. Burke, I am Mr. Beal's man servant, Mr. Duffy."

"Man servant?" Walter said.

"Yes, sir," Mr. Duffy said. "If you permit me, I shall take you to your room where you can freshen up before dinner."

Walter followed Duffy through a maze of rooms and up to the second floor to a bedroom large enough to hold a dozen men. The bed itself could hold six or more. Besides the bed, there was a dresser, chairs, a desk, a large dressing mirror on the closet door and a closed door to the left of the bed.

"What's in there?" Walter said of the closed door.

"Open the door and see, sir," Duffy said.

Walter opened the door and was surprised to find a large, sunken bathtub, all white in color. Against the wall was a sink, cabinets and a rack full of towels. Beside the rack was another door.

"And there?" Walter said of the closed door.

"That is a crapper toilet that came all the way from England," Duffy said.

Walter opened the door. It was an indoor toilet that was attached to an overhead box full of water. "I heard of such luxuries, but have yet to see one. How does it work?"

"After you . . . finish, you pull the chain and water from the tank flushes away the waste," Duffy said.

"To where?"

"A sewer."

"And from the sewer?"

"To the East River, I suppose."

"River?"

"I believe so," Duffy said. "Mr. Beal will be home at 6:45 and dinner is served sharply at seven. You have time to freshen up, take a nap if you wish and change for dinner."

"By freshen up, you mean a bath?"

"Yes, sir."

"I suppose I could do with one," Walter said. "Show me how it works."

Turned out, it was fairly simple to operate. There were two faucets—one for hot, the other for cold—and you let them both run to fill the tub with the right temperature water. Duffy suggested something called bubble bath and after Walter tossed some into the water, it produced a thick layer of soapy bubbles.

"If you require assistance, pull that cord beside the tub," Duffy said.

"Assistance with what?" Walter said.

Duffy smiled and left Walter alone to figure things out.

There was a shaving mirror on a swivel mounted to the rim of the tub and Walter shaved while he soaked in the hot, bubbly water. He wondered if Mrs. Ling back home knew of such luxuries.

When he was done, Walter flipped the little lever between the two faucets and the water in the tub drained, he supposed to the East River. After toweling dry, Walter wrapped the towel around his waist and went to the bedroom where he rummaged through his satchel for a clean shirt.

There was a knock on the door and Duffy opened it and entered with an armload of clothes. "I took the liberty, sir, of selecting the proper dinner attire for tonight."

"What's wrong with what I have?" Walter asked.

"Nothing if you were taking a walk through the park," Duffy said and laid out the suit, shirt, tie and shoes on the bed. "However, Mr. Beal insists all guests be properly suited for dinner. I believe I guessed your size correctly. Let's begin with the shirt."

Duffy held the shirt for Walter as he slipped his arms into it. Duffy buttoned it, then added the tie and stepped back to inspect Walter.

"Now the trousers," Duffy said.

Walter grabbed the trousers off the bed before Duffy and said, "I can put on my own pants, thank you."

Walter slipped into the pants and as he tucked in the shirt, he said, "Mr. Duffy, I have a question."

"The trousers are cut to the left, Sir," Duffy said. "If it's uncomfortable, I can . . ."

"About my sister."

Duffy looked at Walter and nodded his head.

"This place, all this fancy stuff, what kind of woman was she?" Walter said.

"Mrs. Beal was quite a lovely woman, highly educated and well liked by all," Duffy said.

Walter glared at Duffy. "That doesn't tell me a damn thing."

"No, I suppose it doesn't," Duffy said.

Duffy turned to the dresser where a bottle of brandy and two small glasses rested on a silver tray. He filled the two glasses and gave one to Walter.

"Mrs. Beal, your sister, first hired me several months after her marriage to Mr. Granger," he said. "That was almost twenty years ago. She felt that Mr. Granger, who was quite absent-minded, could use some help in the gentlemen department. After he passed, I would have left, but she insisted that I stay. I have been with her through two marriages, the birth of her son and her own illness. I watched as cancer ate away at her body. I watched as she faced her own death with more courage than any human being I have ever known. I loved her as my daughter and the moment Mr. William is gone, I shall tender my resignation to Mr. Beal. Have I answered your question, Mr. Burke?"

Walter stared at Duffy. "Yes, yes you have," he said.

Duffy and Walter raised the brandy glasses and downed then in one quick shot.

"Where is the boy?" Walter said.

"He attends private school during the week," Duffy said. "He will be home this Friday evening for the weekend."

"I see," Walter said.

"Allow me to help you with the jacket," Duffy said. "And then I'll escort you to the study to await Mr. Beal."

"What did you mean when you said the trousers are cut to the left?" Walter said.

CHAPTER FIFTEEN

The study was a large room on the first floor that very much resembled the library Walter once visited in Omaha, Nebraska a few years back. A zoning commissioner suggested they study maps of available land for sale and the one place that had a complete collection was the Omaha Public Library, which he found a dry, stuffy place, much like the study. Every little noise in that library seemed to echo like a marching band. Walter had that same feeling now.

Duffy filled a glass with brandy he called a snifter and dipped the smoking end of a Cuban cigar into the brandy, then held a lit match for Walter to light the cigar.

"The brandy enhances the flavor of the cigar," Duffy explained.

"Obliged," Walter said as he puffed on the cigar. "But, I got another question."

"Sir?"

"And for God's sake, stop all this sir business," Walter said. "Call me Walt or even Walter, but all this sir business makes me feel like an old man in a rocking chair."

Duffy grinned. "Joanna used to scold me as well, when I addressed her as ma'am once too often," he said. "What is your question, Walt?"

"Well, I have been in half the rooms in this house and have not seen one photograph of my sister," Walter said. "I was wondering why that is."

"Mr. Beal had us remove them," Duffy said. "The boy is quite delicate and he feels the photographs around the house are a constant reminder of his mother and unsettling to him."

"Delicate, you say?"

"Yes."

"In what way?"

Before Duffy could answer, the sound of the front door opening gave him pause. "That would be Mr. Beal," he said. "I'll show him in if you'll wait here."

Duffy left the study and a moment later, Jordan Beal walked through the sliding doors. "Mr. Burke, I have heard so much about you," he said and extended his right hand to Walter. "It's a pleasure to finally meet you."

Beal was about forty, taller than Walter by several inches, though not as hardy, clean shaven and dressed in business attire. He was handsome enough, but his eyes were not what Walter would describe as trustworthy because they shifted around as he spoke.

"Mr. Beal, as you can imagine, I have a great many questions," Walter said.

"Come, we'll talk over dinner," Beal said, "where I'll do my best to answer your questions. Allow me a moment to change jackets."

As if on some prearranged schedule, Duffy appeared with Beal's dinner jacket, helped him off with one and on with the other.

"Shall I tell Alice you are ready for dinner, Mr. Beal?" Duffy said.

"Quite," Beal said.

Duffy escorted Beal and Walter to the formal dining room on the first floor. The table was large enough to hold fourteen, but just two places were set. Alice served the first course, a soup made of Swiss chard, something Walter had never heard of before, much less tasted.

"As I had no knowledge my sister was sick, her death came as quite a shock," Walter said as he sampled the soup. He found it tasteless, like eating boiled spinach leaves in a bowl of salted water.

"I can imagine," Beal said. "It was the way Joanna wanted it. She felt her illness and her death were a private affair and I respected her wishes."

Walter nodded. "My sister was, as a child, the sort who kept things close to the vest. I imagine she was the same as an adult. She didn't suffer much at the end, did she?"

"No," Beal said. "We had the best doctors in New York at her care and they provided the medicine to quell her pain so that she eased into her final days without suffering much at all."

"I'm thankful for that," Walter said.

Alice arrived at the table.

"Would you prefer chicken or fish for the second course, Mr. Burke?" Beal asked.

"Never cared for fish much," Walter said.

Alice nodded, went to the kitchen and retuned with baked chicken for the second course. "Ring when you're ready for the salad," she said.

"Ice cream for dessert, Mr. Burke?"

"What's ice cream?" Walter asked.

"A luxurious treat," Beal said. "Alice, we'll take ice cream and coffee in my den."

The den occupied a third of the second floor of the house. It was filled with bookcases, a desk, a long sofa covered in leather with matching chairs, a long table and bar, and something Walter had never seen before. On a smaller desk was a glass dome that contained a brass motor of some sort. There was a slot in the dome with a long train of paper hanging out of it.

Walter studied the dome as Alice served them dishes of ice

cream and hot mugs of coffee. "I have to confess, I am completely baffled by this . . . I don't know what to call it," Walter said.

"That is a very ingenious and valuable device called a ticker-tape machine," Beal said. "As an investment banker, it allows me to get stock quotes almost immediately instead of employing a runner, which can take hours to receive information. I have several of them at my office downtown, but I find one in the house most valuable."

"I won't pretend to know what you're talking about," Walter said. "But, tell me, have you a telephone?"

"Three," Beal said. "One in the bedroom, one in the master kitchen and one here in my den."

"Can I see one?" Walter said.

"Best eat your ice cream first before it melts," Beal said.

Walter dug his spoon into the vanilla ice cream and placed it in his mouth. "I have to admit, this is good," he said.

"They say in another ten years, you will be able to buy it in stores instead of making it at home," Beal said. "And available in many flavors."

"I guess you can say that about a great many things," Walter said. He eyed some framed photographs on the wall. "I see by your pictures that you served during the war."

"I was quite young and served as a junior officer under Grant," Beal said.

"Myself and my two partners sat out the first three years of the war," Walter said. "We joined in late sixty-three when Lincoln made his plea to the country for manpower. We served with Sherman on his march to the sea and were discharged in late sixty-six."

"It's a small world, Mr. Burke," Beal said.

"Well, sir, I have finished my ice cream and I would sure like to see your telephone," Walter said.

"Absolutely," Beal said and stood up. "Accompany me to my desk."

Walter followed Beal to the massive desk that rested beside a window. To the left of the desk, mounted to the wall was a walnut case of which a tiny knob was attached.

"Open the case," Beal said. "Use the knob."

Walter grabbed the knob and pulled and the door of the case, which was on hinges, slid open to reveal the telephone inside.

"It's the latest model for home use," Beal said.

"How does it work?" Walter said.

"Pick up the receiver attached to the cord," Beal said. "You hold that to your ear while you speak into the mouthpiece at the base. Go ahead, try it."

"You mean talk to somebody?" Walter said.

"Crank the handle and wait for the operator to pick up and ask her for the correct time," Beal said.

Walter lifted the earpiece and held it against his right ear. "Crank the handle, you say," he said, and spun it several times.

"Now just wait," Beal said.

Three, maybe four seconds passed before a female voice said, "Operator, how may I direct your call?"

Walter was momentarily taken aback. "Ma'am?" he said.

"How may I help you, sir?"

"I . . . can you tell me the time?" Walter said.

"The time is 8:20 P.M., sir," the operator said. "Do you wish to place a call?"

"No, ma'am," Walter said. "Thank you."

"Goodnight," the operator said and clicked off the line.

Walter replaced the earpiece and closed the lid. "I won't deny that I am somewhat amazed by this," he said.

"By 1890, half the country will be on the telephone," Beal said. "By 1900, almost every home will have at least one or more. It will change America forever."

"What will they come up with next?" Walter said.

"The electric light bulb, Mr. Burke," Beal said, "is the way of the future."

"The what?" Walter said.

"Let's finish our coffee," Beal suggested. "Along with a brandy and cigar."

Walter took a chair while Beal fetched two Cuban cigars from the desk. He gave one to Walter and lit it off a wood match, then lit his own with the same match and took a seat in the other leather chair.

"Mr. Beal, my sister wrote in her letter that I need be present for the attorney to read her will," Walter said. "Do you know why?"

"Actually, I don't," Beal said. "I guess we will find out tomorrow morning."

"I must confess that I am bit taken aback by the wealth my sister acquired," Walter said. "She wrote me often enough, but rarely spoke of money. Do you know how she came by all this?"

Beal puffed on his cigar, took a sip of brandy and said, "Her first husband was a very successful businessman in men's clothing. When he died, she inherited the business and all its wealth. She sold it for considerable profit and invested some of it in various enterprises that paid dividends. In addition, I am a very successful investment banker. When we married, I invested some of her wealth and tripled it over the years. My guess is the boy will inherit most of Joanna's assets."

"I see," Walter said.

"Simply put, Joanna was a wealthy woman," Beal said. "And tomorrow when we meet with her attorney, we will find out just how much."

"And the boy?"

"I'm sure he will be well taken care of," Beal said.

"In San Francisco?" Walter said.

"From what I understand, that is her wish for William," Beal said. "Well, my usual custom is to review the stock quotes on the ticker-tape for an hour or so before bed. Would you care to join me or shall I inform Duffy to ready your bed."

"It's been a long day," Walter said. "I believe I'll say goodnight and turn in."

"Good night, Mr. Burke," Beal said. "I'll see you in the morning."

CHAPTER SIXTEEN

"Duffy, it's a hard time for me," Walter said. He was seated in one of the chairs in his bedroom, a brandy in hand.

"I understand, sir," Duffy said. He was in the other chair, and at Walter's insistence, joined him with a brandy.

"I told you to forget all this sir nonsense," Walter said. "I told you Walter or Walt will do."

"Very well, Walter," Duffy said.

"Let me ask you a right uncomfortable question," Walter said. "Do you trust this Jordan Beal?"

"Let me answer that by saying I already told you I would be giving my notice the moment young William is on the train," Duffy said.

Walter nodded and took a sip of brandy.

"I've heard stories from Joanna that you are something of a gunfighter, Walter," Duffy said. "Quite famous out west. Almost as famous as Buffalo Bill and his Wild West Show. I escorted William to his show last spring, as I recall. It was quite exciting, a spectacle to watch."

"That pipsqueak," Walter said.

"You know Mr. Cody?"

"Twenty-five years," Walter said. "We rode together on the Pony Express. He always was one to brag about himself even when there wasn't worth spit to brag about. He always said he would be more famous than the President one day and I guess he made good on his brag."

"His show is in town, at the Madison Square Garden," Duffy said. "We could stop by and say hello, if you'd like. William won't be home until early evening."

"Bill in the big city," Walter said. "Sure, why not. I expect that lawyer won't take up too much time."

"Excellent," Duffy said. "I shall phone the Garden first thing in the morning."

"Wild West Show," Walter said and took another sip of brandy. "Here in the city where they won't even ride a horse except for fun."

"I should like to see the western frontier someday," Duffy said.

"Well, don't wait too long," Walter said. "To hear Beal tell it, before long, we'll all be sitting on the porch, eating ice cream and talking on the phone to check our stock quotes."

"Walter, I have something for you," Duffy said and stood up. "I will be right back."

Duffy left the room long enough for Walter to roll a cigarette. Just as Walter struck a match, Duffy returned with a thick book and handed it to him. "These were her favorites," Duffy said.

Walter looked at the book on his lap.

"I'll say goodnight, Walter," Duffy said.

"And goodnight to you, Duffy," Walter said.

Alone, Walter opened the book and the first page simply read, Our Family Album. He turned to the second page and stared at the black and white photograph of Joanna at age sixteen, dressed as a proper young woman in school attire. There were photographs of Joanna and her beau Wilson Granger in the park, at the circus, on the steps of a church. Wedding pictures from Chicago. Walter in his dude suit, looking awkward and silly, and so young. Pictures of William shortly after he was born, Joanna holding him in her arms. Family outings, picnics in the park,

Joanna and Wilson in a rowboat, Christmas and Thanksgiving holidays.

Walter felt tears well up in his eyes and he closed the book.

"Some gunfighter you are," Walter said aloud. "Crying like a baby with an empty stomach."

CHAPTER SEVENTEEN

The lawyer's name was Preston Sinclair, and he had a fancy office on Park Avenue about a mile south from Joanna's residence. Duffy drove the one-horse carriage through the streets while Walter and Beal sat on cushioned seats and watched the city roll by them at a snail's pace. It would have been quicker to walk, but Walter kept that opinion to himself.

The trip took about forty minutes to complete as Duffy had to constantly stop at crosswalks and intersections for people to cross. It was an interesting way to see the city and Walter thought the people of New York City always seemed to be in one big hurry to get where they were going or coming from. Most of the men, Walter noticed, wore an expression of stress on their faces, probably from the pace they lived by.

Sinclair's office was in what Beal called an office building. Ten stories high, Beal explained that the only occupants of the building were attorneys and accountants. Walter thought it a waste of space, but he also kept that opinion to himself.

Sinclair was about fifty and had a round belly well hidden inside a gray suit. His hair was thin, hands soft, his voice calm and collected.

After handshakes, Sinclair took his seat behind his desk. "Can I get you anything, coffee or tea?"

Walter and Beal declined.

"All right then, let's begin," Sinclair said and tore open a long envelope that had been sealed with wax. "Before I proceed,

98

do you have any questions?"

"No, sir," Walter said. "Not at this time."

"If I may, when was the will finalized?" Beal asked.

"One month before she passed," Sinclair said. "Prepared in her bedroom by me in the company of her doctor, who pronounced her of sound mind. It was then filed in the courts and sealed for this reading."

"Thank you," Beal said. "Proceed."

Sinclair perched reading glasses on his nose and cleared his throat. "The will in itself is quite simple, although the transactions will require much paperwork. All stocks, bonds, investment holdings and cash assets are to be left to Joanna's surviving son William Granger Junior in the form of a trust fund until he reaches the age of eighteen. The home located on 66th Street and Fifth Avenue is to become the sole property of Joanna's second husband, Mr. Jordan Beal. Mr. Duffy, employed by Mrs. Beal, is to receive one year's salary as compensation for his longtime, faithful services. Papers are necessary to complete the transaction for the home, Mr. Beal. They are ready for your signature."

Beal stayed motionless in his chair. Walter glanced at him and Beal appeared slightly pale in the face.

Walter cleared his throat and said, "I have no right to any of my sister's wealth, and I would refuse any left to me, so I was wondering why it is necessary I be here for this reading?"

"You received Joanna's letter asking you to escort her son to San Francisco?" Sinclair said.

"Yes, sir, I did," Walter said.

"Joanna has allocated twelve thousand dollars in expense money for you to take the boy west to San Francisco," Sinclair said. "I have the cash in my safe for you to take with you when you leave here today."

"Twelve thousand . . . all it takes is a train ticket and three weeks' time," Walter said.

"William is a . . . sickly boy, Mr. Burke," Sinclair said. "Joanna felt it best to have the cash with you on the trip and not need it, than to need it and not have it. Mr. Beal, if you're prepared to sign documents, I shall turn over the rights to the house to you this morning."

"Is Mr. Burke still needed here?" Beal said.

"As soon as I give him the expense money, he can leave," Sinclair said.

Beal looked at Burke. "I can walk to my office from here if you'd like Duffy to ride you home or take a tour of the city."

Ten minutes later, his jacket pocket stuffed with cash, Walter met Duffy at the carriage alongside the curb.

"Shall I drive to the Garden?" Duffy said. "Mr. Cody said he is most anxious to see you."

Walter climbed aboard the carriage. "Why the hell not? This day can't possibly get any worse than it already is."

Duffy drove the carriage south to 26th Street, and then turned west to Madison Square where the Garden building was located. The building was an immense square with a tall tower at the front of the structure where people entered and exited through a large gateway.

A long banner hung from the tower. *Buffalo Bill Cody's Wild West Show featuring Annie Oakley and Frank Butler,* the banner read.

From the carriage, Walter read the banner. "Still blowing his horn," he said.

"I'll park the carriage and we can enter through the back door," Duffy said. "Mr. Cody is expecting us."

Walter and Duffy left the carriage and walked around the wide city block to the rear entrance that was used by staff and stage acts. A uniformed policeman, armed with stick, whistle and .32 revolver, guarded the door.

"This is Mr. Walter Burke, an old friend of Mr. Cody," Duffy told the policeman.

"Mr. Cody told me to expect you," the policeman said. "I'll take you to his dressing room."

The policeman led them through a maze of hallways to a bank of doors marked Dressing Rooms. A large gold star with Bill Cody's image centered in it hung over the first door. The policeman opened the door and Walter and Duffy entered the dressing room.

Bill stood on a footstool while a tailor put the finishing touches on his new spangled jacket and shirt. Twin, silver-coated six-guns were encased in ornate holsters. His graying hair was worn past his shoulders and his chin whiskers made him, in Walter's opinion, look like an aging billy goat.

Bill smiled and brushed away the tailor, then stepped down off the stool.

"Walter Burke, it's been too long," Bill said, extending his hand.

"Howdy, Bill," Walter said. "I see that you have made good on your pledge to be the most famous man in the country."

"Not quite, but there is still time," Bill said. "Come, let's walk. I'll show you around the Garden."

"This here is Mr. Duffy," Walter said. "He is in the employ of my sister."

"Greetings, Mr. Duffy, we spoke on the telephone," Bill said. "Come on, Walter. Let me give you the nickel tour."

Bill led them back to the hallway to the end where it funneled out to the massive interior of the garden.

"Ten thousand people will be here in three hours to see the show," Bill said.

Walter looked around at the long stacked rows of seats that surrounded the main circle of the field where the show would unfold. Indians practiced trick-riding their horses. Cowboys performed fake fights. Calvary soldiers practiced getting shot. Center stage, Annie Oakley set up a table for her trick-shooting performance.

"You've met Miss Oakley?" Bill asked.

"Several times, but not recent," Walter said.

"She is a big part of the show, Walter," Bill said. "Her trick-shooting act brings the house down."

"Still shooting playing cards backwards with a mirror," Walter said. "I remember when she did that back in Dodge for whiskey money."

"She demands a bit more than that these days, Walt," Bill said.

"And what's going on there?" Walter said. "The Indians?"

"We are doing Custer's Last Stand, an exciting reenactment of the true massacre at Little Big Horn," Bill said.

"Sounds like quite an eventful show you got here, Bill," Walter said. "I'm surprised you don't got Wyatt Earp and Calamity Jane here with you."

"Don't think I haven't asked them," Bill said. "Wyatt went west to seek his fortune in gold with that new wife of his, and Jane took to the bottle after Wild Bill met his doom."

"Sorry to hear that about Jane," Walter said. "Our paths crossed but a few times, but I liked her fine spirit."

"Say, you know, Walter, you could do quite well joining my show," Bill said.

"As what?" Walter said.

"As what you are, the genuine article," Bill said. "Do not repeat what I say, but my cowboys are stage actors. I had to teach them to ride and shoot. And my Indians there, they wouldn't know one end of a tomahawk from the other if I threw one at them. They came out of Maine, mostly. Most of them are farmers. Even have that funny accent. You, on the other hand, would bring true western realism to the east. We could do a Pony Express ride, that time you took a Paiute arrow in the back. Or that time you shot it out with members of the Wild Bunch in Utah and killed four of them by yourself. You'll be famous worldwide."

"Worldwide?" Walter said.

"After this season, plans are underway to tour Europe," Bill said. "We will perform for Queen Victoria in London, England, next year."

Walter glanced at Duffy, who was looking at Walter with a strange expression on his face. "Bill, I am just passing through," Walter said. "Taking my sister's boy west to live in San Francisco with his family."

"I'll pay you one hundred and twenty five dollars a week, Walter," Bill said.

"Thank you, Bill, but me and my partners are set to start our own cattle ranch just as soon as I return," Walter said. "Remember Slicker and Sweetwater?"

"I do, and I'll go as high as a hundred and fifty a week," Bill said. "You'll be a rich man and think of the times, Walter. Things are changing rapidly. We have to keep up with them or our memories fade away."

"So people keep telling me," Walter said. "But, Bill, I will try to hold onto the past for just a while longer and save the ice cream and fading for my old age."

Bill stared at Walter for a few seconds, then he sighed and smiled. "To be perfectly honest, Walter, I'd rather be out west with you. I mean, look at this jacket. I feel a fool in it, but the dudes expect to see me in it because they don't know any better."

Walter extended his right hand. "I'll see you, Bill," he said. "Try not to let that jacket get caught in nothing."

Back at the carriage, Duffy climbed aboard his seat. Walter

looked back at the Garden, at the giant banner, then climbed up next to Duffy. "I ain't much for being pampered, Duffy," Walter said. "I'll ride up here with you."

Duffy guided the horse into heavy street traffic.

"So your sister said," Duffy said. "She said you had the kindest heart of any man she'd ever known, but she'd rather face an angry rattlesnake than cross paths with you when you got your burr up. At the time, I didn't really understand what she meant. I do now."

"Well, don't let it bother you none," Walter said. "And to tell you the truth, maybe Alice could teach me how to make ice cream."

"It isn't really that difficult," Duffy said. "You start with ice, sugar and cream."

CHAPTER EIGHTEEN

Late in the afternoon, Walter stood on the sidewalk in front of the house and rolled a cigarette. As he struck a match and lit the smoke, Beal came up behind him.

"My wife, your sister, was a wise woman," Beal said. "I am fond of the boy, but she knew that my work keeps me away from home far too much to be a good stepfather to him. I imagine Joanna's relatives from her first marriage are much more suited to raise the boy than I am."

"Than both of us, I expect," Walter said.

"I imagine I will sell the house as it is far too much room for just one person," Beal said. "I will find a small residence closer to my work. It's best all the way around for everybody."

"I expect so," Walter said. "What time will the boy arrive?"

"Depends upon traffic, but Duffy should have him here within the hour."

"I have a favor to ask," Walter said. "Before we leave on the train, I would like to visit my sister's final resting place."

"Certainly," Beal said. "I'll have Duffy take you there first thing tomorrow."

"Obliged."

"If you'll excuse me, I have some work to catch up on," Beal said. "I'll see you and the boy at dinner tonight."

Walter nodded. Beal returned to the house. Walter finished the smoke and tossed the spent paper into the street. Behind him, he heard a noise and turned to see Alice working in the garden.

"Good afternoon to you," Walter said.

"And to you," Alice said.

Walter started to roll another cigarette.

"May I ask you a question, Mr. Burke?" Alice said.

"Why not," Walter said as he dug out his tobacco pouch.

"Are you a man of patience?"

"I wish I could say that I was, but I am not," Walter said. "I wasn't blessed with that virtue, although I do try."

"Then you will have one very long ride to San Francisco," Alice said.

"I don't understand."

"You will," Alice said. She looked past Walter to the street. "I do believe that is Mr. Duffy with William."

Walter looked to his left and Duffy came along the street and parked the carriage at the curb. In the back seat, William stood up and slowly stepped down to the curb.

Walter stared at the boy.

"It's a virtue as you said, Mr. Burke," Alice said from the garden. "So I've heard."

Dressed in a suit jacket with tie and hat, William wore short pants that came to his knees. Pale and thin, he weighed barely a hundred pounds. He stopped and looked up at Walter. "Are you my Uncle Walter?"

"What in the living hell are you wearing, boy?" Walter said.

"My school uniform, sir," William said.

"Where's the rest of your pants?" Walter said.

"These are shorts, sir," William said. "The required school uniform of summer as the classrooms get quite hot and uncomfortable."

Duffy said, "I shall take the carriage to the livery and return directly."

"My mother said that you are a real cowboy," William said. "Is that true?"

"I will try to live up to your expectations of a real cowboy," Walter said.

"I have no expectations, sir," William said. "I've never seen a real cowboy."

Walter stared at the boy. "Let's go in the house," Walter said. "It's getting close to suppertime."

As they passed the garden, Alice said, "It truly is a virtue, Mr. Burke."

Walter opened the front door and he and William entered the house. At the base of the staircase, William said, "I have to change for dinner. Mr. Beal is very insistent on proper dinner clothing."

"Yeah, he is," Walter said as William dashed up the stairs to his room.

An hour later, Walter, William and Beal converged in the dining room for dinner. William wore a gray suit with long pants and a short paisley tie. Walter wore the suit Duffy provided the night before. Beal wore a black dinner jacket with patches on the elbows, matching pants and tie. Walter thought the jacket more resembled a robe for sleeping than a jacket for eating at a table.

Alice served vegetable soup for the first course, which, while thin to Walter's liking, at least had some flavor to it.

"So, William, are you excited about your trip?" Beal said.

William set down his spoon and dabbed his lips with a linen napkin before answering. "It's what Mother wanted," he said.

"Yes, but are you excited?" Beal persisted. "A new city, school, friends, an entire new world for you to learn."

"Yes, sir," William said.

Alice came in with the second course of roasted lamb.

"I'm told by Mr. Duffy, there is a train scheduled to leave at four tomorrow afternoon," Walter said. "Does that give me time to visit my sister?"

"If you get an early start, you will have adequate time to make the train," Beal said. "William, I'll have Duffy assist you packing your bags after dinner."

"Yes, sir," William said.

"Good," Beal said. "I'll see you off first thing in the morning because I plan to spend the day at the office."

"Sir, will I be able to get my medicines in San Francisco?" William said.

"I wouldn't worry about that, William," Beal said. "San Francisco is a fine, big city with many hospitals and doctors. And your uncle will take excellent care of you on the trip."

"Yes, sir," William said. "Sir, if I may be excused, I'd like to start packing."

"Very well," Beal said.

William stood up. "Good night, sir. Goodnight, Uncle Walter."

After William left the room, Walter looked at Beal and said, "The boy is very polite."

"Yes," Beal said. "Yes, he is."

CHAPTER NINETEEN

Walter and William sat in the carriage while Duffy drove them from Manhattan to The Bronx by a connecting bridge across the Hudson River. Walter noticed that as they drove north through Manhattan, the island was more countrified, with open fields and some dairy farmland, and without so many houses in plain sight.

Once they crossed the bridge into The Bronx, the landscape was green rolling hills and farmland for many miles. Then, in a dramatic shift, the farms gave way to massive mansions and a huge, flat green field that Duffy said was a golf course. Walter heard of the game, but had no idea how it was played. He asked Duffy and was told that the game is played with a tiny white ball and clubs. The object of the game was to hit the ball into selected holes with as few swings of the clubs as possible. The game, Duffy explained, originated in Scotland and was brought over by British soldiers for recreation in the seventeen hundreds.

"Sounds like a foolish waste of a man's time," Walter said.

"The wealthy of Manhattan have built summer homes in The Bronx where land is plentiful and available," Duffy said. "They bring their choices of entertainment with them. Golf or pony polo."

"It's right pretty country, anyway, this Bronx," Walter said. "A right fitting resting place for my sister."

"Mother and I talked about it before she died," William said. "She told me I needed to be strong for her if she were to leave this world in peace."

"My sister was a wise woman," Walter said.

"Mr. Duffy, may we stop for a moment?" William said.

"What for?" Walter said.

"I have a weak bladder, sir," William said.

"Duffy, find the boy a tree," Walter said.

Duffy pulled off the dirt road and stopped at a large oak tree. William jumped down and went to the tree. He stood motionless for a few seconds, then turned around. "I can't go if you watch," he said.

"Duffy, avert your eyes," Walter said.

Walter and Duffy looked away while Walter relieved himself. When the boy climbed back aboard the carriage, he opened the bag beside him and removed a small canteen of water and a cloth to wash his hands.

"Well, if nothing else, I guess you're clean," Walter said.

Less than a mile down the road, Duffy drove the carriage through an iron archway and into the cemetery. It was a massive, well-manicured plot of land, with many headstones made of marble and granite.

"I've seen many a boot hill, but nothing like this place," Walter said as Duffy drove the carriage through the cemetery.

"Boot hill is where they bury the outlaws," William said. "I read that in the Buffalo Bill dime novels."

"Buffalo Bill dime novels?" Walter said. "Why doesn't that surprise me."

"We are here," Duffy said. He stopped the carriage. "Down this row."

Walter and William stepped down from the carriage. William led Walter down the long row to Joanna's headstone. It was a large, ornate marble stone, highly polished. The words, *Joanna Burke, wife of Wilson, mother of William, sister of Walter, daughter of James and Josephine,* were carved into the marble and polished to a darker color.

"Mother selected the words herself," William said.

"Mighty pretty words," Walter said.

"Should we say a prayer?" William said.

"You go ahead and say some words if you want to," Walter said. "Right now I'm a mite testy with the man upstairs for taking my sister at such a young age. If there weren't a boy around I'd speak my mind to him."

"You shouldn't blasphemy, sir," William said. "Mother said blasphemy is a sure way for a man to lose his soul."

"I won't fault her there," Walter said. "Go on and say your words."

William recited the Lord's Prayer while Walter stood with hat in hand.

"I suppose I shall do as you asked, Joanna, and take the boy to San Francisco," Walter said when William finished the prayer. "It's the least I can do having failed you as a brother."

"How did you fail Mother, sir?" William said.

"That is between your mother and me," Walter said. "If you're ready, let's go. We have a train to catch."

"Yes, sir," William said. "I'm all packed and ready to go."

"Glad to hear it," Walter said.

After the drive back to Manhattan and a quick lunch, William said goodbye to Alice, who shed a tear as she hugged the boy on the sidewalk. "Mind your uncle now on the trip," Alice said.

"I will," William said.

"Where is he?" Alice said. "Mr. Duffy has the carriage all loaded."

"He wanted to use the telephone one more time," William said.

A moment later, Walter came out with his lone satchel and walked to the curb where Duffy was securing the last of Walter's eleven bags in the carriage.

"What's all this?" Walter said.

"My belongings, sir," William said. "Just the necessary immediate. The rest will be sent to me by train once we reach San Francisco."

"The necessary immediate?" Walter said. "Son, I've never owned this many belongings in my entire life much less the necessary immediate."

"Yes, sir," William said.

"I'm afraid that you'll have to ride up front with me," Duffy said.

Walter and William climbed up and sat with Duffy. The ride to the train station took about an hour as street traffic was heavy with carriages. At the curb outside the train depot, Duffy stepped down first and said, "I'll get a man to take the luggage. I won't be but a moment."

Walter and William stepped down and stood beside the carriage. Walter rolled a cigarette and lit it off a wood match. Before the cigarette was spent, Duffy returned with a porter, who wheeled a large luggage rack.

The porter looked at the carriage. "How many?"

"Just me and the boy," Walter said. "These are his necessary immediates."

The porter examined the carriage full of luggage. "This is way too much for your sleeping car," he said. "I suggest you take what you need and I'll check the rest into the freight car. You can access it on stops if need be."

"That will do fine," Walter said. He looked at William. "You?"

"Yes, sir, I suppose so," William said.

Walter brought down his lone satchel. William selected two bags of clothing and a small, black bag that resembled a doctor's bag.

As the porter loaded the rest of the bags onto his rack, Walter and Duffy shook hands.

"I suppose Joanna knew what was best for the boy," Duffy said.

"I believe so," Walter said. "You take care."

Duffy extended his right hand to William. "You mind your uncle now."

"I will, sir," William said.

"I'll send word when we reach San Francisco," Walter said.

"I took the liberty of putting a small gift in your satchel," Duffy said.

"I appreciate it and all you've done for my sister and the boy," Walter said.

Duffy watched as Walter and William followed the porter into the station. When they were gone from his view, he sighed heavily and climbed aboard the carriage.

CHAPTER TWENTY

Walter awoke from a nap when a train conductor knocked on the door to his sleeping car and announced the dining car was open for dinner. He sat up on the bunk and looked across the cramped car at William, who was seated in a chair with his nose buried in a book.

"What's that you're reading?" Walter said.

"*A Tale of Two Cities*, sir," William said. "By Charles Dickens."

"Your mother give you that book?" Walter said.

"Yes, sir. She was very fond of Charles Dickens," William said. "She used to read him to me when I was a baby."

"And now you're what, a man?"

"No, sir."

"I suggest we do as the man said and head on over to the dining car," Walter said.

"Yes, sir," Walter said and set the book aside and stood up.

"At least you're wearing pants," Walter said.

William grabbed his doctor's bag and followed Walter out of the sleeping car. They walked from car to car to the dining car, which was quickly filling up with passengers. Against a window, they found a table for two.

After a few minutes, a waiter came to the table.

"What's in the kitchen tonight?" Walter said.

"Baked chicken, New York steak, breaded lamb chops, all served with vegetables," the waiter said.

"I'll have the steak, well done and with coffee," Walter said.

"And the boy?" the waiter said.

"The baked chicken, sir," William said. "And do you have milk?"

The waiter nodded. "It will be about fifteen minutes."

There was a pitcher of water and two glasses on the table. Walter filled both glasses, then busied himself rolling a cigarette.

Walter opened his bag and began removing tiny pillboxes, which he set on the table in front of him.

"What's all this?" Walter said as he struck a match.

"My medicines and pills, sir," William said.

"For what? What ails you, boy?" Walter said.

"Many things, sir," William said. He reached for a pillbox. "This one is for my asthma. It helps to prevent attacks."

Walter pointed to another pillbox. "And that one?"

"For my bones."

"Your bones? What's wrong with your bones?"

"I'm fragile, sir," William said. "The doctor said these pills will help strengthen my bones and prevent them from fracture."

Walter blew a smoke ring. "I don't think I care to know the rest."

"Yes, sir."

After dinner, Walter had a slice of apple pie for dessert with coffee. William asked for rice pudding, a dessert his doctors said was good for his bone density because of the high calcium content.

"Density?" Walter said. "What's that?"

"Thickness," William said.

"I see," Walter said.

With dessert consumed, Walter said, "I believe I will head to the gentlemen's car for a cigar, brandy and some conversation. You're welcome to join me, boy."

"Thank you, sir, but I think I will return to the car and read a few more chapters before bed," William said. "Cigar smoke gives me headaches and clogs my sinus passages."

Walter stared at the boy. "Suit yourself," he said.

In the gentlemen's car, Walter sipped a brandy, smoked a cigar and engaged in conversation with some men from Chicago who traveled to New York to see Buffalo Bill's Wild West Show.

"Most exciting," one of the men said. "Six-guns blazing, Indians falling from their horses, I could barely catch my breath. Have you seen the show?"

"I have not," Walter said.

"You must see it the next chance you get," the man said. "I understand that next year, it will be touring Europe and performing for the Queen."

"And the horsemanship is amazing," another man said. "Where does a man learn to ride a horse like that?"

"Not in Chicago, that's for sure," the first man said.

The group thought that funny and laughed.

"If I may ask," Walter said. "What do you men do in Chicago?"

"We're in the cattle business, sir," the first man said.

"You're ranchers?" Walter asked.

"Heavens, no. We own and operate the new slaughterhouses where the cattle are butchered for market," the second man said. "Why, I've never even ridden a horse in my life and I don't think I care to," he laughed.

"I see," Walter said. "Well, goodnight, gentlemen. I'm sure I will see you all again."

Walter took his leave and returned to the sleeping car. It was dark when he entered and he struck a match to light a lantern. As he started to undress, he looked at William, when the boy moaned in his sleep.

Walter bent over William and saw that the boy was drenched in sweat. He felt William's forehead and it was hot to the touch with fever.

Walter went to the dining car, which was now closed, but some workers were about cleaning up. "I have a sick boy," he said to a kitchen worker. "I wonder if you have some crushed ice and water I can have."

Walter returned to his car with a bucket of crushed ice and a pitcher of water. He took a facecloth off the rack by the wash basin, dipped it in the ice water, then the crushed ice until the ice stuck to the cloth and then folded it.

Walter removed the covers from William and washed the boy's face with the ice-cold cloth. He did this several times, then dipped the cloth in the water and ice again and set it on William's forehead.

It took about an hour of repeating the process, but finally the fever broke and William began to shiver from the cold. Walter covered the boy with the covers and an extra blanket, then sat to roll and smoke a cigarette. Finally, Walter removed his clothes, extinguished the lantern and went to bed.

About an hour passed, during which time Walter tossed and turned. He gave it up, got out of bed and struck a match to the lantern. He remembered then Duffy's gift and reached for his satchel and opened it. Mixed in with his clothing was a pint bottle of expensive French brandy.

"Duffy, you're a man after my own heart," Walter said as he removed the cork and took a swig of the brandy.

There was something else peeking out between his shirts. Walter grabbed it and was shocked to see it was the journal he'd given to Joanna nearly twenty-five years ago the night before she set sail for New York.

"My God," Walter said softly. He set the brandy on the floor and opened the journal. He glanced at William, then reached for his spectacles in the satchel and put them on. Joanna wrote on the first page, *This book given to me by Walter, my brother, on the day I got on the boat for New York.*

Walter flipped the page. *I hid behind a large woman so Walter couldn't see me crying. I'm 14 and I didn't want him to believe his sister to be a crybaby at my age. I watched him cross the street and go into the Pony Express office. A man in a white jacket told me I had to go inside to the desk, so I left and went inside.*

The rest of the page was blank and he turned to the next. *I didn't write nothing for three days because I have been sick with what the doctor on the ship called seasickness. I have been throwing up a lot and am dizzy all the time. The doctor said it was from the swells of the ocean. He said I would get used to it and I did. I'm feeling much better now, thank you for asking.*

Walter found himself grinning as he flipped the page. From that page until the very last, Joanna wrote of her exploits aboard the ship, bound for New York, as she put it. He sipped the brandy, rolled cigarettes and read every word of every page.

Joanna described the first calls of port in San Diego and then all the way down to Baja California where they picked up and let off passengers and took on supplies. *Baja is pronounced BaHa, on account of it's a Mexican word and they have no H in their alphabet like we do in American. There is a man who works on the ship named Jesus, like the baby Jesus, but he says his name is Hesus, because he is Mexican. He told me so.*

As he continued to read, Joanna described her stops in South America, at such places as Colombia, Ecuador and Peru. She spoke of the many people she met and the friends she shared meals with. She said it was sad to see them leave, but new people always took their place, so there was always somebody to talk to and share stories with. Most of the men talk of the war they believe will come shortly, and the women talk of clothes, homes and family.

When in port in Peru, she wrote, she saw natives on land that were very strange to look at. *They were almost naked and had their bodies painted in bright colors, and wore strange things in their ears and noses. I was told they are Indians, but they look nothing like the Indians back home.*

Joanna described the long voyage around South America and then north along its coast to Mexico and finally to the coast of Florida where they stopped in the city of Miami for repairs to a sail.

From Miami, the ship sailed to Atlanta, Washington D.C., Philadelphia and finally to New York City. *When the ship slowly sailed to the port in New York and I saw the city from a distance for the first time, there was an excitement in my heart I could only describe as the time when I was seven, before Mama died and I received a new doll for Christmas.*

The one sadness I feel knowing as I leave the ship is that it will be many years before I see my brother Walter again.

Footnote: I had much help writing this story from many kind people on the ship as my writing and spelling is not very good at this time. I hope to learn much and improve in the future.

Walter closed the journal and sat quietly for a while on his bed. He rolled and smoked another cigarette and sipped brandy while he smoked it. He heard William roll over and he looked at the boy.

"You best be worth it," Walter said softly.

CHAPTER TWENTY-ONE

Walter sipped coffee and watched as William set out his pills on the table in the dining car.

"Don't you never run out of pills, boy?" Walter said. "We been on this train a week and it seems like all you ever do is eat pills."

"I made sure to pack enough to last the entire trip, sir," William said.

The waiter arrived with plates of eggs, bacon and toasted bread with butter.

William started to swallow his pills with water.

"I was reading them papers that lawyer gave me to give to your relatives in San Francisco," Walter said. "If I done my figuring right, you stand to get almost three hundred thousand dollars from my sister in cash alone."

"Yes, sir," William said as he took a final pill. "Mother and I read the papers together, along with Mr. Sinclair."

"You understand them?" Walter said.

"Yes, sir."

"Maybe before this trip is over, you could explain them to me. Eat your breakfast before it gets cold."

Walter and William dug into the eggs.

"You had another fever last night," Walter said. "Third time in seven nights. How come you have such?"

"There was a breakout of scarlet fever at school," William said. "They said it was from being in such close quarters that it spread and infected many of the boys."

"Scarlet fever?" Walter said. "You got that from school?"

"Yes, sir."

"Well, the warmer climate of San Francisco will do you some good."

"Mother said that, sir. So did my doctors."

After breakfast, Walter and William went to a riding car where Walter read a newspaper and William dug out another book.

Walter glanced at the cover through his spectacles. "What happened to Dickens?"

"I finished it, sir. This one is by Jules Verne, called *Around the World in 80 Days.*"

"By the size of it, it will take eighty days to read it," Walter said.

A conductor came through the car and Walter waved the man over.

"What's our next stop?" Walter said.

The conductor pulled out his pocket watch. "Dodge City in two hours," he said. "There will be a one-hour layover to take on water and coal. You're free to step off provided it's not for too long."

"Thank you," Walter said.

The conductor nodded and walked away.

"I believe I'll go have a cigar," Walter said to William.

"Yes, sir," William said without looking up from the book.

"Go to our sleeping car once I leave," Walter said.

"Yes, sir."

Walter went to the gentlemen's club for coffee and a cigar. He joined a conversation about the chances of Grover Cleveland winning the presidency. Another group of men were discussing an invention they read about in the newspaper, the diesel engine, which ran on fuel made from crude oil.

"They say it will change the world," a man in the group said.

"How so?" Walter said.

"They say it will replace the horse one day as man's primary means of transportation," the man said. "By using the engine to power the wheels of a wagon, the wagon will no longer need a horse to pull it. They say in fifteen years, everyone will ride a horseless carriage instead of the back of a horse."

"Who is they?" Walter said.

"The newspapers."

The conversation returned to politics and Walter quickly grew bored, finished his cigar and returned to his car where William was on his bed, still engrossed in his book.

Walter sat on his bunk and rolled a cigarette. He felt the train slow its speed. He lit the cigarette and by the time it was finished, the train rolled to a gentle stop in the depot.

Walter stood up. "Come on, boy, we're going to stretch our legs."

"You mean get off the train?" William said.

"That's what I mean."

"Why, sir?"

"Because I had enough of eastern dudes with their horseless carriages, and whiny children with their pills," Walter said as he grabbed his satchel.

Walter took William by the hand and pulled the boy along the hallway to the car where they could exit the train. They stepped out to the wood platform where Dodge City sprawled out before them just a short distance away.

"Come on, boy," Walter said and dragged William down the steps to the dusty street that was dotted with piles of horse manure.

"Take a look, boy," Walter said. "This is a real town."

William's eyes scanned the dust-filled streets, the plank wood sidewalks, the buildings constructed mostly of wood with a few made of red brick, the men on horseback, the women in western clothing. A thousand sights, smells and sounds filled his head all at once and made him dizzy.

"This is not good for my sinuses," William said.

"Come on," Walter said and yanked the boy up to a wood plank sidewalk. "Before you step in something you shouldn't."

"Where are we going, sir?" William said.

"Never mind," Walter said. "Smell that air, boy."

"I can't, sir. My sinuses are getting clogged."

"Call me sir one more time and I swear to God, I will spank you like a baby right here on Main Street," Walter said. "Call me uncle or Walter or both, but not sir. Understood?"

"Yes, Uncle," William said.

"Now, come on," Walter said and led William down the long plank wood sidewalk. They crossed the street and Walter came to a dead stop.

"Damn," Walter said.

"That's a bad word, sir. I mean, Uncle. Mother said . . . ."

"Never mind what your mother said. I see a man coming I'd rather not see at the moment and don't you use such words until you're at least eighteen," Walter said.

"What man, Uncle?"

"Him." Walter pointed.

William looked at a U.S. marshal as he strolled toward them, tipping his hat to ladies on the street. The marshal wore black pants with a white shirt and black vest. His badge glistened when it caught the sunlight. A .45 Colt was in a worn holster on the right side of his waist below the hip. He paused and grinned when he caught sight of Walter and William.

"Well, the jig is up now," Walter said. "That is Marshal Bat Masterson. Come on, boy, let's get it over with."

Walter led William across the street where Masterson grinned and shook his head at them.

"I had to look twice to see if that was really Walter Burke or the church preacher I was seeing," Masterson said.

"William, this is U.S. Marshal Bat Masterson," Walter said. "Bat, my sister's boy William from New York City."

"New York, eh," Masterson said. "That's why the dude clothes."

"Thought I'd fit in," Walter said.

"Did you?"

"No."

"Where you bound for?" Masterson said.

"Taking the boy to San Francisco to live with family."

"I plan to go there one day myself," Masterson said. "Become a newspaper man like I always wanted to."

"I don't have much use for newspapers at the moment," Walter said.

"Say, Walt, I could use another deputy around here," Masterson said. "My brothers got a big territory to cover and the cowboys come in on payday and you know how it goes."

"I surely do, Bat, but I got to take the boy west and after that, me and my partners are starting up our ranch," Walter said.

"Where about?"

"Ain't rightly sure just yet," Walter said. "My partners are in Lincoln working on the details."

"Let me know if you change your mind," Masterson said.

William looked up at Masterson. "Are you the Bat Masterson I read about in the dime-store novels, sir?"

"Don't believe everything you read, son," Masterson said. "I hate canes and never owned a derringer. Much of what you read I made up to give the reporters back east something to jaw about. Your uncle here, he is the real thing, though."

"Yes, sir," William said.

"Well, Bat, I have to send a wire to my partners," Walter said. "Maybe I'll see you later for a drink."

Masterson looked at Walter. "Don't let him give you any of his bad habits, son."

"Yes, sir."

Walter and William continued on down the street.

"What bad habits, Uncle?" William said.

"Never you mind that right now," Walter said.

Walter paused in front of the Western Union telegraph office. "Wait here," he said. "I'll only be a minute."

William stayed on the sidewalk while Walter entered the telegraph office. Men on horseback rode by and they seemed giants to him on their tall steeds. No one was dressed as the cowboys in Buffalo Bill's Wild West Show, he noticed. They lacked tan coats with dangling frills and their horses had no silver buckles in their well-worn saddles.

"What are you looking at, boy?" Walter said when he came out.

"The horses, Uncle."

"Ever been on one?"

"No, Uncle."

"Dressed as we are no self-respecting animal would have us on their backs," Walter said. "Come on."

"Where to, Uncle?"

"There," Walter said and pointed to a large mercantile store across the street.

They crossed the street and entered the store. It was one giant room sectioned off in various departments, clothing, tools, supplies, weapons and housewares. A man wearing a white apron came around the counter to greet Walter and William.

"Morning, gents," the man said.

"Morning," Walter said. "Me and the boy need a set of trail clothes, boots for the boy. We also need forty-pound saddlebags, cookware and chaps."

"You're talking some money, friend," the man said.

125

"Money I got," Walter said. "Trail clothes and supplies I don't."

"Got some right nice trail clothes in black right over here," the man said and led Walter and William to the men's clothing section. "Hats, too."

"I'll keep my hat, but the boy needs one," Walter said.

"Uncle, I don't understand why I need these clothes," William said.

"It's simple, boy," Walter said. "We ain't in New York no more. Ain't no fancy pants going to carriage you around. Find your size, or as close to it."

"You can change in those rooms over there," the man said.

Ten minutes later, Walter emerged from a changing room wearing black pants with a matching black shirt. He kept his belt and hat and carried the satchel to the counter where the man waited.

"I need a Winchester rifle for the ride as well," Walter said. "And a few boxes of ammunition for it and my .45 pistol. What do you got for trail knives?"

William emerged from his changing room wearing his new black trail clothes, boots and hat. "I feel silly dressed like this, Uncle," he said.

"Maybe you feel so, but you don't look so," Walter said. He turned to the man. "Pick out two saddlebags and fill them each with forty pounds of supplies. Coffee, beans, canned goods, flour, sugar, jerky and fill two three-gallon canteens with fresh water. Need two bedrolls as well and grain for two horses. I'll pay you now and be back directly."

"Say two hundred dollars and we'll call it even," the man said.

Walter counted out two hundred dollars from the expense money and set it on the counter. "If I think of anything else, I'll let you know when we return. Keep an eye on my satchel for me."

"These boots hurt my feet, Uncle," William said.

"Come on, boy," Walter said. "Your feet will survive, I might not."

"Where, Uncle?"

Walter nudged William out the door to the plank wood sidewalk.

"Livery stable," Walter said.

"But, Uncle, the train?" William said.

"Hang the train," Walter said.

"I don't understand," William said.

"Which is exactly your problem."

Several blocks away was a large livery with corral and barn. Walter and William entered and found a man at a desk in a small office.

"Can I help you, friend?" the man said, getting up from the desk.

"Need two horses," Walter said. "A tall male for me, a small mare for the boy, both broken and the mare gentle. No nags, they got a long ride. I need two saddles, nothing new. Don't have time to break them in."

"Let's take a look out back," the man said.

Walter and William followed the man through the barn to another corral behind it where horses for sale were penned.

"That large male with the white spot is three years old and in his prime," the man said. "Across the pen, that mare is perfect size and temperament for the boy."

"I'll take them both," Walter said.

"Do you have three hundred dollars cash money?" the man said.

Walter counted out three hundred from the expense roll. "I expect you to throw in two blankets and brushes for free."

"I'll saddle them right up," the man said.

Walter and William returned to the front of the livery where Walter paused and rolled a cigarette.

"We're missing the train, Uncle," William said.

Walter pulled out his pocket watch. "No, we missed it," he said.

"All my things," William said.

"Will arrive in San Francisco where your people will pick them up," Walter said.

"And what am I supposed to do about . . . ?" William said.

The man came out with the saddles horses. "Here you are, sir," he said. "Saddled and ready to go."

"Grab the reins, boy," Walter said. "We'll walk them back to the store."

William took the reins for the mare from the man.

"That's it," Walter said. "You walk, she'll follow."

Walter led his horse along the street with William and the mare behind them. In front of the store, Walter tossed his reins around the hitching post. "Just loop it around like I did," he told William. "She won't go nowhere."

William looped his reins around the post.

"Wait here, I'll be right back," Walter said.

Walter entered the store where the man was waiting for him behind the counter. "Everything is packed and ready to go," the man said.

Walter quickly inspected the saddlebags and bedrolls. "Fine job," he said. "Now if you will get a pouch of tobacco, papers and matches, I'll be all set."

Walter carried one saddlebag and his satchel to the street, the man carried the other. "Come again next time you're in town," the man said.

Walter slung the saddlebags over the horses and tied them down, then inserted the Winchester rifle into its long holster.

Then he opened the satchel and removed his holstered .45 Colt and slung it around his waist.

William watched his uncle put on the massive Colt handgun. It struck William that the moment his uncle was armed, he became an entirely different man. No longer his grouchy uncle, but a man to be feared and respected.

"Let's go, William," Walter said.

"Sir. Uncle, I've never been on a horse before," William said.

"No, I expect you haven't," Walter said. "We'll walk to the marshal's office and then walk the horses to the end of town. That way, you'll have less to be embarrassed about when you appear so foolish."

"But, Uncle, I really need my . . ." William said.

"That's the end of it," Walter said. "Young children such as yourself are best seen and not heard unless directly spoken to."

Walter took the reins of his horse and walked toward the marshal's office. William slowly followed behind. When they arrived at the office, Walter looped his horse and said, "Wait here, I won't be but a minute."

Masterson was at his desk when Walter walked into the office. "That's more like the old Walt," he said of Walter's new trail clothes.

"I decided to take the boy by horse the rest of the way," Walter said.

"That's about a 1,200-mile ride, Walt," Masterson said. "If you don't mind me saying, the boy doesn't look up to the mark."

"He better be," Walter said. "Listen, I would like you to send two telegrams for me first thing tomorrow. One to my partners in Lincoln, the other to the boy's family in San Francisco."

Masterson slid a sheet of paper and pencil across the desk. "No problem, Walt," he said. "I'll take back the favor next time you're in town. I'll pin a badge on you."

CHAPTER TWENTY-TWO

Walter and William walked their horses to the very last street in Dodge City, then turned west and continued until they reached the fringe of where the prairie met the town.

"This is as far as we walk," Walter said. "Mount up."

"Sir, I mean Uncle, I have never been on a horse before," William said.

"You said that," Walter said. "Don't say it again, because the moment you climb onto that saddle, it will no longer be true."

With one quick motion, Walter placed his left foot in the stirrup and eased up onto his horse. "Nothing to it," he said.

William stared at the stirrup for so long, Walter said, "Just exactly what do they teach you at that fancy-pants school in New York?"

"Mathematics, history, geography, science, English, and many other subjects," William said. "Reading is my favorite subject."

"None of which will do you any good in your present situation," Walter said. "Now unless you can convince that horse to read and you write a letter asking her to take a bow, I suggest you climb aboard so we can get moving."

William looked up at his mare, placed his foot in the stirrup and slowly, painfully climbed into the saddle.

"Take hold of the reins," Walter said. "When I move out, your mare will automatically follow."

Walter yanked on his reins and his horse moved forward and William's mare followed closely behind.

"Where are we going, Uncle, and why did we leave the train?" William said.

"Where we are going is a town in Wyoming called Laramie, or just north of it," Walter said. "And why we left the train is because I can only take so much eastern dudes at one time and besides, no kin of mine is going to grow up a dandy."

"What's a dandy, Uncle?" William said.

"Next chance you get, look in a mirror," Walter said. "Now come on, I'd like to make twenty miles before we break for nightfall."

Walter rode his horse at a constant, even pace suited to the flat but rough terrain, keeping William's mare slightly behind him at all times. Since the boy didn't ask to stop, he didn't and they made close to twenty miles by late afternoon.

Walter didn't see one man on horseback the entire afternoon, although he picked up sets of horseshoe prints and some mule deer. The sun was low on his back when he stopped his horse and turned in the saddle to look at Walter. The boy was pale and at some point had been crying for his eyes were red and his cheeked streaked with dry tears.

"This is as far as we go today," Walter said as he dismounted. "We'll get an early start in the morning."

William stopped his mare but didn't move to dismount from the saddle.

"Get down, boy, we got things to do before dark," Walter said.

"I can't, Uncle," William said. "My legs are cramped and my back is stiff."

Walter grabbed William by the shirt and yanked him to the ground, where William cried out in pain as he sat on the ground.

"Quit cry-babying and gather up some wood for a fire while I tend to the horses," Walter said.

William slowly stood up and arched his back. "Wood?"

131

"Yeah, wood, unless you want to eat a cold supper," Walter said.

Sniffling, William wandered off to gather some wood. Walter removed the saddles, saddlebags and blankets from the horses and brushed them down before giving them their evening grain. He wouldn't give them water as they would graze on grass after the grain. If they passed a stream or pond tomorrow, he would allow them to drink.

William returned with an armload of sticks and twigs.

"That will do to start the fire," Walter said. "We'll need another six armloads to make the night and try and find some big pieces with dry bark on them."

"I don't think there's enough wood out there for six more armloads, Uncle," William said.

"Look in my saddlebag for a small camp ax," Walter said. "Chop if you have to."

"Yes, Uncle," William said.

Walter dug a round hole six inches deep with the camp shovel included in the gear he purchased at the mercantile back in town. He surrounded the hole with rocks to ward off the breeze and then filled the hole with dried grass and leaves and covered them with the wood. He placed several wood matches under the wood and struck a match and lit leaves and grass to ignite the wood.

By the time William returned, Walter had a nice fire going. "Another load and she'll be hot enough to cook on," he said.

"Yes, Uncle," William said and took off again.

Walter filled one of two frying pans with some water and beans, another with strips of bacon from the ten-pound salted bag, and set them to cook. He filled the metal coffee pot with water and coffee and placed that directly on the fire to boil. While the food cooked and coffee boiled, Walter dug out his new knife and started whittling the bark off the firewood.

When William returned with another armload, he was pale and gasping for breath.

"Sit a while," Walter said. "That might be enough."

William sat in front of the fire, which made him appear even paler. He looked at the coffee pot. "I'm not old enough to drink coffee, Uncle," he said. "My doctor said I need milk for my bone density."

"Those doctors tell you when to wipe your backside?" Walter said. "You'll find a couple of cans of condensed milk in the saddlebags. Mix it with water in your cup; it thins out to a drinkable level. Your bones should be happy."

"Yes, Uncle," William said. "Uncle, why are you removing the bark from the sticks?"

"Bark burns hotter than the wood," Walter said. "Before we turn in, I'll set all the bark in the fire to get it burning hot, then add the wood so it will burn late into the night and we can keep warm in our bedrolls around the fire. I'll save some of the bark to start a new fire in the morning. I think our supper is ready."

"I'm not hungry, Uncle," William said.

"I don't care if you're hungry or not. You eat or you stand guard duty all night," Walter said.

"Guard duty against what, Uncle?" William said.

"Bandits, wolf, coyote, Indians, rattlesnake, puma, take your pick, boy," Walter said. "They're all out there and they love to eat spoiled, rich city boys."

"That isn't true," William said. "You're just trying to frighten me."

"No? Stay awake and find out," Walter said. "In the meantime, we eat."

Walter filled two metal plates with beans and bacon and gave one to William. "Get your milk if you want. Otherwise drink water."

William wasn't the least bit hungry. His entire body ached

from head to toe and he felt weak and dizzy from the long ride. Also, his hands were red and sore from the ax. However, he took the plate and spoon and ate what he could, washing it down with warm water from his canteen.

After eating, Walter cleaned the pans and plates by boiling water in a cup and pouring it over them to sterilize them so they would be ready for the morning.

"Get your bedroll," Walter told William.

William got his bedroll and set it by the fire. Walter put the dry bark on the fire and when it burned hot enough, he added the rest of the wood. Then he got his bedroll and spread it out, rolled a cigarette and sat to smoke it by the fire.

"You sleep good, boy," Walter said. "Come morning, you'll need all your strength, believe me."

"Yes, Uncle," William said and turned away from Walter so that his uncle wouldn't see him cry himself to sleep.

CHAPTER TWENTY-THREE

William opened his eyes to the sound of a crackling fire. It was barely light out, just minutes after dawn. He smelled coffee and bacon. He rolled over and felt the stiffness in his back, the soreness in his legs and the pain in his very stiff neck. He sat up and looked at Walter, who was seated by the fire, smoking a cigarette.

"Morning, boy," Walter said. "I thought you might sleep the day away. Get up and have some breakfast. I have store-bought biscuits I got back in town."

William crawled out of the bedroll and sat beside the fire. He seemed pale and feverish. Walter tossed his cigarette into the fire and looked at William. "What is your ailments, son?" he said.

"You know of my asthma," William said. "I also suffer from low red blood count, ulcers in my stomach and on occasion, I suffer from severe headaches. I have weak bones and require a daily dose of Vitamin C."

"Bones again, huh," Walter said. "What is it with your bones?"

"Sir, Uncle, I feel quite ill," William said.

"That's because you don't eat enough to fill a starving prairie chicken," Walter said. "Grab a plate and some of these biscuits. They won't last another day or two at best, so we might as well eat our fill of them now."

"Yes, Uncle," William said.

"And grab a can of that condensed milk," Walter said. "What you don't drink, I'll put in my coffee."

William went to his saddlebags for a can of the milk and returned to the fire. "I have nothing to open it with," he said.

Walter took the can and used his knife to stab through the top. He splashed a dollop of the thick milk into his coffee cup and gave the can back to William.

"Now eat," Walter said.

William loaded a few slices of bacon and two biscuits onto his tin plate. He filled his tin cup with condensed milk and added water to thin it out. He took a bite of a biscuit and washed it down with milk.

"If we encounter no surprises on the trail today, I'd like to make thirty miles or more by sundown," Walter said.

"I don't think I can do that, Uncle," William said. "I am so sore that I can barely walk."

"You'll do it or fall from the saddle trying," Walter said. "Besides, I ain't asking you to walk."

William was suddenly sniveling and Walter was taken aback by the boy's crying.

"By God, no," Walter said.

"No, what?" William said in between sobs.

"A couple, three years back, me and my partners made a stop in Little Rock to pick up a wanted man," Walter said. "We had a two-day wait for the federal papers to arrive and we took in a show at this playhouse they got there. This woman singer from back east sang what they call opera. Didn't understand a word she sang all night. After the show, she talked to folks in the lobby. She had this little poodle dog in her arms. It was pink and cut to look like a cotton ball. Had a pink bow and its nails were painted to match. That's what you remind me of, a little pink poodle dog."

"There is no need to be cruel to me, Uncle," William said.

"Cruel?" Walter said. "The only thing missing from you is the pink bow and painted nails. If you ask me, my sister was the one cruel to have raised her son to be the way you are, a dandy."

"My mother said you'd— . . ." William said and caught his tongue.

"Your mother said what?" Walter said.

"Nothing, Uncle."

Walter set his empty plate aside and started to roll a cigarette. "I won't pretend to know these ailments that seem to afflict you. I ain't that smart. But, I do know this. Whatever they are, they will have to wait until we ride into San Francisco. The same for the spoiled, rich boy, nipple to the grave life you will live once we get there. Is that clear?"

"Yes, Uncle," William said.

"Finish your breakfast," Walter said. "No man worth a spit is in bed after sunrise, and that includes you."

The sun was shifting across the sky to early afternoon and they hadn't made good time on the trail. Thirty miles was out of the question. They would be lucky to make twenty by nightfall. Walter was hesitant to open his horse up for fear of the boy falling off his. He kept it at a slow but steady pace.

"I think we should noon here and rest the horses a bit," Walter said. "Okay with you, boy?"

William didn't respond and Walter turned around in the saddle to look at him. The boy was hunched over, passed out cold.

Walter dismounted and stopped the boy's mare. William fell from the saddle into Walter's arms. "Yeah, here is a good spot," Walter said.

Walter put the boy in the shade of some tall brush and built a campfire. While the beans and bacon cooked and the coffee boiled, he wiped William's face with a wet cloth and slowly the boy came around and opened his eyes.

"Did I fall asleep?" William said.

"More like passed out," Walter said.

William sat up. "I'm sorry, Uncle," he said. "I didn't mean to pass out. The sun was so hot on my back."

"Well, come and eat," Walter said. "Nothing worse than an empty stomach on a long ride."

William stood up and walked to the campfire. "My legs and back ache so much, I can barely walk," he said.

Walter sat and filled a plate with beans, bacon and biscuits. "The first rule of being a man is to never sound like a complaining woman. Eat."

Walter took a bite of a biscuit and realized just how hungry he was when he barely chewed it.

"Second rule is to live by your word," Walter said. "Once given, you break it for no man or no reason."

"You gave your word to take me to San Francisco," William said.

"I gave no such word I would do it by train," Walter said. "Once we get there you can do as you please. Grow up to be one of them big-bellied bankers for all I care, but no kin of mine is going to whine like a pigtailed schoolgirl over riding a horse, no sir. Not while I draw breath. Now eat. We have miles to make up before sundown."

Late in the afternoon, the sun was an orange ball, low in the sky. To Walter's surprise, William kept pace, slow as it was, and they made up a bit of time they lost in the morning.

"What do you think, William?" Walter said. "Does this look like a good spot to make camp?"

"I guess so, Uncle."

"You guess so," Walter said. "Would you know a good spot from a bad one?"

"No, Uncle, I wouldn't."

"Tell you what," Walter said. "I'm in the mood for some

roasted chicken. How about you, boy?"

"I'm not sure I understand, Uncle," William said.

"No, huh," Walter said. "Climb down and hobble your mare."

"What's hobble, Uncle?"

Walter dug a four-foot section of rope from his saddlebags and tossed it to William. "Tie her front legs together so she can't run," he said. "Not too tight, just so she can't take a step."

"Why, Uncle?" William said as he dismounted.

"I'll show you why after you hobble her."

William looped the rope around his mare's front legs and tied a knot in the rope. "This is called hobbling, Uncle?" he said.

"Yes, now fetch a couple of good-sized stones to throw," Walter said.

"Throw at what, Uncle?"

"Our supper," Walter said.

William searched the ground and found a couple of medium-sized stones.

"Now, on your left, see that big clump of sage brush?" Walter said. "On my count of three, toss them stones into it."

Walter pulled his .45 Colt and cocked the hammer.

"One . . . two . . . three," Walter said.

William tossed the stones into the brush. A dozen or more prairie chickens came scurrying and flying out. Walter fired one shot into a chicken, cocked the hammer and fired a second shot into another. The noise of the shots was deafening and William covered his ears for the second shot as his mare bucked a bit but couldn't run off because her legs were tied.

"Go pick up our supper, boy," Walter said. "We got some cleaning to do."

While Walter plucked the birds and gutted them for the spits he made of long sticks, William gathered rocks and built a fire. By nightfall, the chickens were close to roasted, the beans bubbled in a pan and Walter sipped hot coffee.

"Break out your knife and fork for the chicken, boy," Walter said. "And the salt and pepper from the saddlebags."

A few minutes later, Walter placed an entire chicken onto a plate, spooned in some beans, added a biscuit and gave it to William. "You'll do well to finish all that," Walter said.

William sliced into the breast and hot juices flowed down the bird and mixed with the beans. "How did you know the birds were in that brush?" he said.

"Birds like to nest in shade," Walter said. "Only shade around here is in brush."

"What if you missed?" William said.

"Missing never occurred to me," Walter said. "If you don't want that biscuit, pass it here."

William sloshed the biscuit in the beans and took a bite of it and as he chewed, he smiled at Walter. "It's good," he said.

"I do believe we'll make Colorado by tomorrow nightfall," Walter said. "We should reach a town to resupply before then, pick up a pouch of biscuits and corn dodgers and some other possibles."

"After we eat, should I gather more firewood?" William said.

"I'll do that," Walter said. "Maybe it's your turn to wash the dishes."

William nodded. "Can you shoot as well as Buffalo Bill Cody?" he said.

"Well, there's shooting and then there's shooting," Walter said.

"I don't understand," William said.

"It's one thing to shoot at cards and pie plates backwards with a mirror," Walter said. "The pie plate don't shoot back. It's another thing to shoot at a man when he's shooting back at you. Most ain't got the stomach for it. They blink or draw a breath and some just freeze up with fear. I seen a lot of that in the war. And another thing, it ain't as important to be fast as it is accurate."

William nodded. "I would like to try shooting," he said.

"Unfortunately, I have nothing light enough with me you can handle," Walter said. "But, if you're serious, I can pick up a nice .32 pocket pistol for you to practice with until you fill out some."

William nodded. "I best see to the dishes."

Walter stood up. "Well, the wood ain't gonna bring itself," he said and went off to gather firewood.

CHAPTER TWENTY-FOUR

The sun was just about ready to show itself when Walter opened his eyes to the sound of bacon sizzling in the pan and the smell of boiling coffee in the pot. He sat up in his bedroll and looked at the campfire where William was stirring the bacon with a fork.

William looked at Walter. "Someone told me a man ain't worth spit if he's still in his bedroll after sunup," William said.

"Since you're in such a good mood, I believe we'll do forty miles today," Walter said as he stood up. "And those beans are boiling over."

Walter and William rode side by side for four hours, stopping once to fill their canteens at a stream and to allow the horses to drink.

"Uncle, how come you let the horses drink sometimes and other times you don't?" William said.

"The horse ain't exactly what you would call a smart animal," Walter said. "They don't know the difference between being a little thirsty and dying of thirst. If you let them drink their fill all the time, they cramp up and hurt themselves. Can even die from it. If there's sweet grass around, they're better off filling up on that as it's mostly water anyway, and they absorb it slowly. Any more questions?"

"Yes, this country looks different, Uncle," William observed when they remounted.

"Kansas is flat as a pancake," Walter said. "Colorado is mountain country. A lot greener with mud every spring and fall when the snow melts and runs down the Rockies below. The farmers like it, the ranchers don't."

"What you said to the marshal back in Dodge City about your ranch," William said. "Where will you build it?"

"That's what we're going to Laramie to find out," Walter said.

"Uncle, look there in the distance," William said.

"I see it."

"What is it?"

"Let's go find out."

They rode for about a quarter mile and stopped a hundred yards from a covered wagon, wheels deep in mud. A man was pushing hard against the back, while two boys and a woman pulled from the front.

"They have no horses, Uncle," William said.

"Only way you get mud like this is from heavy rain," Walter said. "My guess is their horses ran off during the night afraid of lightning and thunder."

"Should we help them?" William said.

"Ride in slow," Walter said. "A man gets jumpy when he believes his family is being threatened."

The man behind the wagon noticed Walter and William riding in and he stopped pushing against the wagon and reached inside for a heavy plains rifle. The woman and two boys came and stood behind him.

Walter and William stopped their horses a safe distance from the man.

"Good weapon, a plains rifle," Walter said. "I carried one during the war. Only problem is it won't fire when the powder's wet. Did you reload after the rain last night? Me and my sister's boy saw your wagon stuck there in the mud and thought we could be of some help. You don't need to be pointing that thing at us, we mean you no harm and like I said, damp powder ain't much good anyway."

The man stared at Walter and slowly lowered the rifle. "Sorry, mister," he said. "We're alone out here and . . ."

"No need to apologize for protecting your family," Walter said. He dismounted and looked at William. "Think you can ride my horse so we can get these folks out of the mud?"

"Yes, Uncle," William said.

Walter walked his horse to the front of the wagon. The man walked with him.

"My name is Kendrick, John Kendrick. That's my wife Susan and our two boys John and James."

"Glad to know you, Mr. Kendrick," Walter said. "I'm Walter Burke and that runt is my sister's boy, William."

"Our horses run off last night when a quick storm blew in without warning and the thunder and lightning spooked them," Kendrick said. "And you are right. I didn't check the powder this morning."

Walter hooked his horse to the hitching rains, turned and looked back at William. "All right, boy, take my horse. Me and Mr. Kendrick will push and when I say go, you ride hard until we're clear."

William dismounted his mare and stood before Walter's tall horse. He was at least two feet higher than William's mare and hundreds of pounds heavier. William placed his left foot in the stirrup, grabbed the saddle for leverage and somehow managed to mount the horse without falling off and appearing stupid before his uncle and strangers.

Walter and Kendrick placed their backs against the rear of the wagon and braced themselves. "Okay, William, pull!" Walter shouted.

William yanked hard on the reins and the horse moved

forward, straining against the weight of the mud-stuck wagon. It seemed like nothing happened, then slowly the powerful horse started to inch the wagon forward until, with a sudden violent yank, it was free and rolling.

Walter and Kendrick, jerked by the sudden quick motion, fell backside first into the mud. Susan Kendrick and her two sons laughed at the sight.

Standing, Kendrick said, "Now Susan, boys, it ain't polite to laugh at company, especially when that company just saved our bacon."

William came running to the rear of the wagon. "We did it, Uncle," he said, looked at Walter and joined in the laughter.

Still seated in the mud, Walter glared up at William. "Give your old uncle a hand, boy," Walter said.

William extended his right hand to Walter, who took it and yanked the boy face first into the mud beside him. "Now we all have something to laugh at," Walter said.

William looked up, his face covered in wet mud, spit dirt and started to laugh. Walter stood and yanked William to his feet.

"There's a stream right over there we can wash in," Kendrick said. "I'd be obliged if you and the boy stayed and had lunch with us."

Walter looked at William. "What do you think, boy?"

William nodded. "I could eat."

Susan Kendrick proved to be a first-rate cook, even from a wagon stove on the open prairie. After lunch, Kendrick and Walter drank coffee and had slices of yesterday's apple pie warmed over the fire, William tossed a ball with James and John in the open prairie.

Susan joined the men after cleaning up the wagon.

"That was a fine meal, Mrs. Kendrick," Walter said as he ate the last bit of pie.

"It's the least we could do for saving us a day's work," Susan said.

"Where are you folks headed?" Walter said as he took out his tobacco pouch.

"We bought a small spread just north of Greenly," Kendrick said. "We come all the way from Wisconsin to buy this spread. We have to meet the bankers in eight days."

"You'll never make that without horses," Walter said.

"I plan to start out first thing in the morning and find them if they haven't wandered too far," Kendrick said.

"Where one goes, the other goes," Walter said. He looked at William, who was tossing a large baseball to John. "Hey, William!" he shouted.

"Yes, Uncle?" William said.

"Think you can saddle our horses?" Walter said.

"Must you go so soon?" Susan said.

Walter stood up and walked toward his horse. "We'll be back before nightfall," he said and grabbed his saddle to help William.

The trail of the runaway horses was an easy one to follow. Their tracks in the deep mud stood out for even a blind man to see and once clear of the mud, the deep impressions in the grass could be seen from a distance of fifty feet or more.

"They took off northwest of here," Walter said. "Probably in a panic and settled down once the rain stopped. My guess is they are resting in a field somewhere."

"Do you think they went far?" William said.

"Too far for a man to track on foot," Walter said. "Horse is a herd animal. Where one goes, they all go, and these two just kept following each other all night until they got tired. If I was to bet, I would say we'll find them standing around grazing on sweet grass somewhere ten miles or so up ahead."

They rode at a moderate pace for about an hour and a half

and then, in a clearing a hundred yards in front of them, were the two horses. Walter slowed his horse to a stop, as did William.

The two horses looked up from the grass they were grazing on and turned their heads to look at Walter and William. They snorted softly and nervously twitched their legs, unsure if they should run or not.

"They spotted us," Walter said. He reached down and removed his rope from its saddle hook. "All horses are skittish, so we'll ride up easy so as not to spook them and when I give the word, I want you to break your mare hard to their left. They will break right and allow me to rope one of them. With one in tow, the other will follow along like a puppy after its mama."

Walter moved his horse forward at a slow but steady pace. William kept abreast of Walter until they were fifty feet from the two horses. As they closed in, the two horses snorted nervously at them.

Walter removed his lasso from the saddle horn.

"Now is the time," Walter said, and broke his horse into a dead run.

William yanked hard on the reins and raced his mare to the left of the two horses. Startled, the horses broke to their right exactly as Walter said they would and they charged directly into Walter's path.

Walter held the lasso above his head in his right hand, swung it several times, then tossed it out and around the neck of one of the horses. He jerked his horse to a stop and the roped horse immediately came to a short, abrupt stop.

The second horse came about and gently stopped beside the roped horse.

"Got one, got the other," Walter told William.

"Can you teach me to throw a rope like that, Uncle?" William said.

"I expect so," Walter said. "A week ago, you never been on a horse and now you're chasin' runaways."

"That was actually fun, Uncle," William said.

"It was at that," Walter said. "Well, let's get them back. I have a feeling Mrs. Kendrick will be making a fine supper for us as a reward."

Walter looped a second rope around the two horses to keep them together for the return trip. By the time they reached the Kendrick wagon, it was close to sundown. John and James Kendrick ran out to greet them.

"Sally, Sam, you bad horses," James scolded the pair.

"Don't be too hard on them, son," Walter said. "They're just being what nature made them to be."

Kendrick took the two horses from Walter. "Caught four good-sized hares Susan's stewing in the pot," he said. "And she baked a fresh pie in the woodstove just for you."

Walter dismounted and said, "My mouth's watering already."

After supper, Susan and her sons retired to the covered wagon while Walter and Kendrick sat and rolled cigarettes by the campfire. Close to the fire, William slept inside his bedroll.

"It's a fine warm evening," Walter said.

"It is that," Kendrick said. "And because of you and the boy, we will make our appointment with the bank. We're in your debt, Mr. Burke."

"That rabbit stew evened things up," Walter said. "And the pie swung it back over to you."

Kendrick struck a match and they lit the cigarettes. "Where are you and the boy bound for?" Kendrick said.

"I'm taking the boy to live with my sister's family in San Francisco," Walter said. "My sister recently left us and the boy's stepfather is not suited to raise him."

"I'm sorry about your sister," Kendrick said. "A boy should

148

not have to grow up without parents. I don't know what I would do if I lost Susan."

"I hope to God you never have to find out," Walter said.

Kendrick looked at William inside the bedroll. "He's a fine boy, Mr. Burke. You must be very proud of him."

"When you put it that way, I guess that I am," Walter said.

With his back to the fire, Walter couldn't see William open his eyes and smile to himself at Walter's comment.

Susan Kendrick stuck her head out of the covered wagon. "Mr. Burke, there is one piece of pie left in the tin. It would be a sin to waste it."

"Seeing as how you classify it a sin, I'll have to agree," Walter said and stood up.

CHAPTER TWENTY-FIVE

"That sure was nice of that Mrs. Kendrick to bake us these corn dodgers and biscuits," Walter said. "We have enough for two more days' ride."

"They are very nice people," William said. "It was a good thing to help them."

"Yes, it was and you remember that," Walter said. "The second rule of being a man out west is to help somebody if you can, because one day it will be you who needs the help. That's a fact out here."

"Yes, Uncle," William said. "How far did we ride so far today?"

"Fifteen miles, maybe," Walter said.

William nodded and bit into a corn dodger, then sipped water from his tin cup. He and Walter sat against their saddles while their horses grazed on sweet Colorado grass. Since leaving the Kendrick family three days ago, they covered close to eighty miles north through Colorado. William found he grew more comfortable in the saddle with each passing mile. His back no longer ached and his legs no longer went numb from the hours spent atop his mare.

"We should reach Greenly by tonight," Walter said. "We'll stock up on supplies, let the horses feed and rest in a livery, sleep in a bed and reach Wyoming by noon tomorrow."

"Then to Laramie?" William said.

"Three days' ride from here at most," Walter said.

William took another bite of his corn dodger, looked off in the distance and fell silent for a minute or more.

"What's on your mind, son?" Walter said.

"I was wondering what happens after we reach California?" William said.

"What happens about what?" Walter said.

"To you?"

"You will go to school and live with your mother's kin," Walter said. "I will finally get to start my ranch after all these years. That's what will happen."

"It doesn't seem fair that Mother left me all this money while you . . ."

"Fair ain't got a thing to do with it, William," Walter said. "My sister did what was right by her only son and that is what she was supposed to do as a mother."

"Why can't you stay with me in San Francisco?" William said. "You could start a ranch out there."

"Ranching days are over out there," Walter said. "It's all about gold, mining and timber and besides, if I change plans at this time, those two hens I'm married to would have fits the likes nobody's ever seen."

"You have two wives, Uncle?"

"And they're more dang trouble than they're worth," Walter said. "Best saddle up before the horses bust a gut eating grass and they wind up riding us."

William wanted to push the issue of two wives, but Walter pressed them hard to reach Greenly, so they rode past normal suppertime, ate what was left of Mrs. Kendrick's corn dodgers and arrived well after dark. The town lights could be seen from quite a distance away and as they rode closer to Greenly, piano music from several saloons carried out to them on the night air.

As they rode onto Main Street, the town was a contradiction in that the street was deserted, but the noise and music from a dozen saloons made it sound like there was a parade going on at high noon.

"The Greenly Hotel serves a fine supper," Walter said. "But, first we livery the horses. Third rule, a man cares for his horse first and himself second. You take care of your horse and it takes care of you. Understand?"

"I do, Uncle."

"Good boy."

Walter carried his Winchester rifle with him as he and William left the livery stables and walked along the wood plank sidewalk to the hotel.

"That piano music, Uncle?" William said. "Who is playing it?"

"Every saloon in every town's got a piano player," Walter said. "Helps the patrons forget how bad the whiskey is they're drinking and how bad their luck is at the card tables."

At the Greenly Hotel, Walter checked into a room with double beds, then he and William entered the dining room and found a table. Although late, they were able to order the house steak with trimmings, pie and whole milk for William.

"They got a fine bath house where we can clean up in the morning after breakfast," Walter said. "I think we both could do with one."

While eating pie after dinner, James Masterson, younger brother of Bat and a full U.S. deputy marshal in his own right, entered the restaurant. He walked directly to Walter's table.

Walter recognized him immediately.

"James Masterson," Walter said.

James sat in the vacant chair next to William.

"This is my sister's boy, William," Walter said. "He met your brother Bat back in Dodge not long ago."

"Hello, sir," William said.

"Hello, boy. Walter, I wish this were a happier occasion," James said. "Two cowboys rounding up strays rode in a few hours ago and said they came across a covered wagon with a murdered family in it. Three men shot the husband, wife and two young boys. They took everything of value from the wagon and the horses and left them out there on the prairie for the pack wolves."

"Name wouldn't be Kendrick, would it?" Walter said.

"It would, according to their family bible those cowboys brought back with them," James said.

"We ran into them three days ago," Walter said. "Had a wheel stuck in the mud. They were headed here to buy a ranch. They were right nice people."

"The man at the livery recognized you and told me you were here," James said. "I'm putting a posse together for the morning. They'll be slowed down with the two extra horses, so I figure to catch them inside of three days. I sure could use you, Walter."

"I have to take this boy to his family in San Francisco, or I'd go with you in a heartbeat," Walter said. "I can't leave him behind and he's too green for a ride like that."

"I understand, Walter," James said.

"When you catch them, hang them for me, James," Walter said. "And for the boy here."

"You can be sure of that," James said.

After James left the table, William said, "May I be excused, Uncle?"

"Go to the room while I fetch some clean clothes from the saddlebags. I'll be along directly."

When Walter returned from the livery with a pouch of clean clothes and opened the hotel room door, he found William on a bed, crying in the dark. Walter closed the door, lit a lantern and sat down on the other bed.

"I know how you feel, son," Walter said. "I feel bad, too, but this country is full of men who would kill you for your boots and others just because they like to see things bleed. It's the way things are and you better get used to that fact or you'll spend your whole life crying into a pillow over things you got no say in."

William rolled over and sat up. "Maybe if we stayed with them, it wouldn't have happened?" he said.

"Maybe," Walter said. "And maybe if we didn't happen by, they would have been killed that day and maybe if they stayed put in Wisconsin, they would all be alive this very minute. *Maybe* is a word usually used for things we want and not things that are. At your age, you have a long way to go and you'll see a great many more things that don't seem fair, but you can't cry for the maybes and do only what you can do for the what are. Understand?"

William wiped his nose and nodded his head. "Yes," he said softly.

"Now we will get undressed and you can say that Lord's Prayer to keep the Kendrick family in His good grace," Walter said.

William nodded and started to unbutton his shirt. "Will they really hang those men?" he said.

"Only if they haven't shot them first," Walter said. "Either way suits me just fine."

William was shocked to hear himself say, "Me, too."

CHAPTER TWENTY-SIX

After another hard day's ride, Walter and William were deep into Wyoming Territory. They covered forty miles that morning into the evening. Late in the day, Walter paused atop his horse and pointed into the distance.

"Those mountains you see that look like tiny hills on the horizon, those are the Colorado Rocky Mountains," Walter said. "Pretty to look at, but deadly to reside in come winter. That high up, winter stays a long time."

"I studied about them in . . ." William said and suddenly started to wheeze and gasp for breath.

Walter turned in the saddle. William was as pale as a new hotel bed sheet. He wheezed, gasped and fell from the saddle. Walter jumped down and grabbed the boy in his arms.

"William, what is it, boy?" Walter said.

Gasping, wheezing, William tried to answer, but could not get the breath to speak.

Walter placed his arms around William's chest and pulled up until William's arms were extended outward. "Relax your throat, boy," Walter said. "Don't try to breathe, just allow the air to seep into your lungs a little at a time."

Walter held William higher under the arms to open the boy's chest and lungs. "Slowly, don't hurry," Walter said. "It will come when it's ready."

William gasped and wheezed for air and as Walter held him up under the arms, air started to return to William's lungs. He wheezed and sucked in small amounts of air and after about ten minutes, his breathing started to return to normal and some color returned to his face.

"I . . . haven't had . . . my . . . medicine in almost a week," William gasped.

"And that's my fault," Walter said. "I should have listened to you when we left the train."

William regained enough strength to sit up on his own. "I should have had the bottle with me instead of in my bag," he said.

"It's this damn thin air," Walter said. "We're a mile or more above sea level. The air gets thin. It even gets to the horses if you run them too hard. I found that out working for the Pony Express."

"You rode for the Pony Express?" William said. "Why didn't Mother ever tell me about that?"

"I don't know, son," Walter said. "I expect she felt hateful toward them for bringing us apart. Can you ride?"

"I think so."

"We pass through Laramie on our way," Walter said. "There's a doc there. We'll stop and get you what you need."

Walter helped William mount the mare, then mounted his own horse and they rode on at a slow pace for a while.

"How did you know what to do, Uncle?" William said.

"My sister was plagued with asthma all her childhood," Walter said. "The doctors said she would outgrow it and she did just that."

"Mother had asthma?" William said. "She never told me."

"I think you'll find as you get older that women are much better than we are when it comes to keeping secrets," Walter said. "Men tend to be bucket mouths when they're bragging and silent when they should be talking."

"Is Laramie a big town?" William said.

"Big enough to have a doctor's office."

"A candy store?"

Walter grinned. "I expect so."

CHAPTER TWENTY-SEVEN

As they rode through an open field of tall grass, Walter paused on his horse and William pulled up alongside him.

"See that cabin down yonder?" Walter said. "I recognize those two horses in that corral."

"Way down the hill?" William said. "With the smoke blowing up the chimney?"

"That's called the lineman's shack," Walter said. "This is the Double R Ranch property and this is their range we're crossing. When their cattle aren't grazing, they open it up to the smaller ranches in the territory."

"What's a lineman's shack, Uncle?"

Walter moved out and William followed. "A lineman, you see, he rides the range in wintertime sort of on patrol for strays, rustlers and pack wolves. He packs food for the winter and lives in that cabin. We did some work for the Rogers family some years back and they let us use the cabin whenever it ain't occupied and we have a need."

"What kind of work, Uncle?" William said.

"A gang of rustlers killed two of their men and stole a hundred head of cattle," Walter said. "Mr. Rogers hired us to find the rustlers and return his cattle."

"And did you?"

"We did."

"What happened to the rustlers?"

"We hung them from the first sturdy tree we came across,"

Walter said. "And left them hanging there as a beware to others with such notions."

William looked at Walter.

"I lost no sleep over it," Walter said. "Move around to the west side of the field. I want to come in behind the cabin."

"Why, Uncle?"

"The best way to rid a premise of bees is with smoke."

"Bees?"

"Never mind, come on," Walter said and broke his horse into a quick gallop.

William followed Walter west down the field until they came up behind the cabin on a soft hill that put the horses' heads nearly even with the slope of the roof. "Watch the chimney," Walter said. He removed his bedroll and gently tossed it atop the stovepipe chimney to block the escaping smoke.

"Come on, boy," Walter said and rode his horse around to the front of the cabin. William followed and they sat atop the horses and waited.

It didn't take long. With the door and window shutters closed, smoke came billowing out from under the door. A few moments later, the door opened and Slicker and Sweetwater rushed out, coughing and gasping for air.

"Are you ladies having a problem with the chimney?" Walter said.

Slicker and Sweetwater looked at Walter. "What kind of no-good low-down snake would pull a stunt like that on his partners?" Sweetwater said.

William laughed out loud at the sight of the two coughing men.

"I'll ask you to mind your tongue around my sister's boy," Walter said.

Slicker and Sweetwater looked at William.

"You be William?" Slicker said.

"Yes, sir," William said. "Are you my Uncle's two wives?"

"What?" Sweetwater said.

"What's he talking about, Walt?" Slicker said. "Two wives?"

Walter dismounted. "He's talking about a long story I'm not in the mood to tell at the moment," he said and walked toward the small corral in front of the cabin where a large mustang munched on oats from a bucket. "What's this?"

"That's Slick forgetting his age," Sweetwater said.

William dismounted and walked with Slicker and Sweetwater to the corral.

"The bronco buster at the Double R couldn't put a dent in this animal's hard head," Slicker said. "They were fixing to put him down, so I figured . . ."

"To take a crack at him," Walter said.

"Why not?" Slicker said. "I broke many an animal just as stubborn as this one."

"More than likely the only thing breaking will be your bones and your stupid neck," Walter said.

"I told him that very thing," Sweetwater said. "But, he will not listen."

"What's on the stove?" Walter said. "Me and the boy are sick of corn dodgers."

"I love corn dodgers," Sweetwater said.

"You're welcome to whatever's left in our saddlebags," Walter said.

"Got beef stew simmering in a pot," Slicker said. "Which we can eat just as soon as you clear out the chimney."

CHAPTER TWENTY-EIGHT

Late in the afternoon, Walter, Slicker and Sweetwater sat in chairs and drank cups of coffee on the front porch of the cabin. William hung on the corral fence and watched the mustang.

"It's a thousand hard miles to San Francisco, Walter," Slicker said.

"I know the distance," Walter said. He took out his tobacco pouch to roll a cigarette.

"The boy's no bigger than a day-old calf," Slicker said. "He don't look up to the mark if you don't mind my say so."

"The boy will surprise you," Walter said. "He surprised me. He made it from Dodge City to here and with few incidents and never being on a horse before in his life."

"All I'm saying is a ride like that is no day at Sunday school," Slicker said.

"You an expert on Sunday school?" Walter said.

"When you fixing to go?" Sweetwater said.

"Day after tomorrow, me and Sweet will head to Laramie for supplies and better mounts for the trip," Walter said. "As soon as we return, me and the boy will head out."

Slicker picked up a pouch beside his chair and removed some long leather strips. He started to braid the strips into rope.

"Now what did you find out from the bankers?" Walter said.

"They said we can afford to buy three spreads outright with what we have," Slicker said. "One here in Wyoming, another in Nebraska and the third up in Montana."

161

"I don't think I want to ranch during a Montana winter," Walter said. "What's your pick?"

"We figure to check out Wyoming and Nebraska first, see what the lay of the land is," Slicker said. "Course, once we buy the property, we don't have anything left for startup money except a few thousand."

"After I cut out one thousand for the trip, I can put ten thousand into the pot for startup money to buy cattle and horses," Walter said.

"That don't seem right you carrying our load," Slicker said.

"I'm not carrying nothing," Walter said. "We're equal partners, and besides, you're doing all the work while me and the boy ride west. It seems a fair trade for all involved."

Slicker nodded as he twined leather strips. "It still makes more sense to take the train than to ride," he said.

"Maybe so," Walter said. "But the boy needs to learn more than they teach in schoolbooks. He needs the kind of education comes only from experience."

"Like we got," Sweetwater said.

"I hope to hell not," Walter said.

"So how was the big city?" Slicker said.

Walter struck a match and lit the cigarette. "Big," he said and blew smoke.

"That don't tell us nothing," Slicker said.

"They got buildings made of stone blocks a hundred feet or more tall," Walter said. "The trains run underground in dug-out tunnels and the homes got the outhouse right inside with a flush toilet. You pull a chain and away it goes. The boy's house had a telephone right inside and I used it."

"You did not," Slicker said.

"Yes, sir, I did," Walter said. "I asked the woman for the time and she told me. It's a scary thing when progress stares you in the face and laughs at you."

"Did you lose your new watch?" Slicker said.

"I did not," Walter said. "I just needed something to say."

"When you pull the chain, where does it go to?" Sweetwater said. "On that flush toilet."

"The East River, I'm told," Walter said.

"The river?" Sweetwater said.

William turned from the corral and walked to the porch. He looked at the strips of leather in Slicker's hand.

"What are you making?" William said.

"Against a spirited animal such as that one, a man needs an edge," Slicker said.

"What kind of edge, sir?" William said.

"You'll see come morning," Slicker said.

"And hopefully, we won't have to bury you come afternoon," Walter said.

"All them people in New York flushing into the river," Sweetwater said. "Don't it get kinda messy after a while?"

"I won't worry none too much, Sweet," Walter said. "I think they got about as much use for the river as they do riding horses."

"They use a filtration system that filters and cleans the water before it reaches the river," William said. "I studied it in school. It's called a leach field."

"I hate leeches," Sweetwater said. "Filthy blood suckers."

William looked at Walter. "What does he mean, Uncle?"

"Only the good Lord knows and he ain't sharing his secrets," Walter said.

CHAPTER TWENTY-NINE

Walter, Sweetwater and William sat in chairs on the porch and watched the sun creep higher in the morning sky. Walter and Sweetwater had cups of coffee. William drank a glass of milk made from mixing condensed milk with water. William noticed how the rising sun cast the plains and mountains in the background in an eerie, orange glow, something he'd never seen in New York as the buildings blocked the view of the sunrise and sunset.

Walter rolled a cigarette and gave it to Sweetwater, then rolled a second one for himself. He struck a match and lit them both.

"That was a fine breakfast of scrambled eggs you made this morning, Sweet," Walter said. "You'll make someone a fine wife someday."

"I don't plan on getting married, Walt," Sweetwater said.

"Where is Mr. Slicker?" William said.

"Around back," Walter said. "Here he comes now."

Slicker came around the side of the cabin wearing chaps over his black pants and carrying the leather reins he wove and a small wool blanket. He walked toward the corral.

"What's he doing, Uncle?" William said.

"Fixing to break that animal," Walter said. "Or his neck."

William stood up. "I want to see."

"We'll all go see," Walter said.

Slicker opened the gate and the large mustang immediately backed away. Slicker closed the gate and slowly walked toward

164

the skittish horse.

"You and me is going to have us a little talk," Slicker said.

Walter, Sweetwater and William arrived at the corral and climbed the first slat for a better look.

Slicker walked to the mustang and it reared up a bit as Slicker patted its neck. "We're going to have this conversation no matter what," he said. "Best set your mind to it right now."

Rubbing the mustang's neck, Slicker gently placed the blanket over its eyes and loosely tied a knot to hold it in place. "Steady, boy," Slicker said. "Nothing I do is gonna hurt you."

Slowly, Slicker placed the bit into the mustang's mouth and attached the leather reins into the holes. The mustang backed up a bit and Slicker rubbed his neck. The massive horse settled down a bit and Slicker gently placed the saddle onto its back and tied it in place.

"When we are through, one of us won't be so prideful," Slicker said.

Slowly, Slicker climbed aboard the saddle. With his eyes covered, the massive mustang didn't move and allowed Slicker to sit atop its back.

"Now show me something," Slicker said and removed the blanket.

Immediately, the mustang bucked. He jumped and bucked around the corral with furious anger as he tried to remove Slicker from his back. Slicker held fast, one hand holding the leather reins, the other held above his head for balance.

As the corral was small, there was no place for the mustang to run and it kicked and bucked and finally smashed through the closed gate, sending Walter, Sweetwater and William running for cover. Bucking over the broken gate, the mustang tripped and went down with Slicker on his back.

Unhurt, the mustang bounced back up more determined than ever to shake his unwanted rider.

"You'll have to show me better than that," Slicker said.

As if responding to Slicker's challenge, the mustang bucked and kicked with violent anger and frustration at not being able to remove Slicker from its back.

"Best not get in their way," Walter said to William.

Walter, William and Sweetwater stayed close to the corral and the mustang kicked and bucked wildly across the front of the cabin. As the mustang neared the cabin, its back legs kicked the water barrel, shattering it. Then it approached the steps and bucked up them to the porch.

"Slick, git that animal down from there!" Walter yelled.

Desperate to remove Slicker from its back, the mustang reared up on its hind legs and smashed through the front door and stormed into the cabin.

"I hope you valued nothing in there," Walter said.

"If he goes out the back wall we won't see our horses for two days at least," Sweetwater said.

There was a great deal of smashing and breaking that took place inside the cabin before the mustang crashed through the front window and immediately jumped off the porch, taking half the railing with him.

"Sweet Jesus," Sweetwater said.

On the ground again, the mustang made a last-ditch effort to rid himself of Slicker. He bucked, kicked and jumped until he was too exhausted to kick anymore and slowly settled down and fell still.

Breathing like a man who just climbed a mountain, Slicker rubbed the mustang's neck. "That wasn't so bad, was it?" he said.

Dripping salty foam sweat, the mustang snorted.

"Let's go back with our head high," Slicker said and gently rode the mustang back into the corral.

"And that's the way it's done, William," Walter said. "If you got the sand for it."

Wide-eyed, slack-jawed, William stared at the mustang and Slicker.

"We best fetch ourselves some tools," Walter said.

"What for?" Sweetwater said.

"Cause the door and railing ain't going to repair themselves," Walter said.

As Walter and Sweetwater hammed out a new door, railing and window for the cabin, William and Slicker stood on the first rail of the corral and watched the mustang. Nervous at being penned, the mustang skittishly looked at them from a safe distance.

Wiping his brow, Sweetwater said, "Why ain't Slick fixing the door? He broke the damn thing."

Walter looked at the corral where William was trying to coax the mustang to come closer. "When you can do that to a wild mustang hell bent on destruction, we will fix the door."

"I suppose you want me to make supper, too?" Sweetwater said.

"I'll tell you what," Walter said. "Seeing as how you volunteered to go with me tomorrow, I'll cook the supper."

"Volunteered to go where?" Sweetwater said.

"Quit talking and work," Walter said. "Before it's dark and nobody eats."

After supper, Walter, Slicker and Sweetwater sat at the repaired table in the cabin and studied an old paper map by lantern.

"I figure a week to reach Rock Springs where I can resupply," Walter said. "I'll buy a mule in Laramie for the trip."

"That's hard country, Walt," Slicker said as he studied the map. "You figure to cut across Idaho and south through Nevada?"

"I'm studying on the best route for resupplying," Walter said. "With a loaded mule and our own saddlebags, we could go two weeks between stops."

"If the flats and desert don't kill you," Slicker said. "Why not go Idaho into Oregon and south to California? It would add two weeks to the journey, but the boy won't have to find out what the desert heat feels like in summer."

"That might be best at that," Walter said.

The cabin door opened and William came in with a lantern. He set the lantern on the table. "I did like you said, Mr. Slicker. All the horses are in the corral, rubbed down with the brush with fresh water and oats."

"He give you any trouble?" Slicker said.

"The big mustang?" William said. "No, sir. He won't come close enough to be of any trouble."

Slicker looked at Walter. "Walt, you want to take him for your ride? He could do a thousand miles without breaking a sweat, that animal. I'll work on training him while you're off getting supplies."

"I would," Walter said. "And the boy?"

"That male you rode in," Slicker said. "I think it would suit him fine for such a long journey."

"What about it, William?" Walter said. "You want to trade up?"

"Yes, sir," William said. "I would."

"Now that we have that settled, there's something else," Walter said. "I expect you to put the time Sweet and I are away to good use. I'll write down a list of chores I expect you to perform and Slick, you see to it he does them."

"What kind of chores?" Slicker said.

"The kind that builds character," Walter said. "Are you gonna argue with me or you going to do as I ask?"

"Of course we'll do as you ask, Walt," Slicker said. "Cause we can't stand listening to you complain if we don't."

"Then let's go to bed," Walter said. "I want to leave for Laramie first light."

CHAPTER THIRTY

With the loaded mule in tow, Walter and Sweetwater crossed the open range on the return trip from Laramie. It was early afternoon with the sun stretched high across the horizon.

"I have to hand it to Slick," Walter said. "That is a fine animal he broke. Can't be more than two years old. He should have tamed him some by the time we get back. I was thinking we could have a side business of supplying horses to the Army along with our cattle. What do you think, Sweet?"

"I'll throw in with whatever you and Slick decide," Sweetwater said.

"I know that," Walter said. "I'm asking what you think."

"Montana, the Dakotas is the best place to raise horses for the Army," Sweetwater said. "On account of the many forts they built to protect the ranchers and settlers. But, it would be a long drive to take the cattle to the marketplace that far north."

"It would at that, however, I was thinking more the smaller cavalry outposts than forts," Walter said. "We'll see what Slick thinks when we reach the cabin."

"We should be there by sundown," Sweetwater said. "If we skip noon, eat in the saddle and keep riding through."

"I expect," Walter said.

They munched on cold biscuits and jerky in the saddle to keep their stomachs quiet as they crossed the open range and close to sundown, they spotted the cabin in the distance about a half mile away.

"Slick better have something decent in the pan or the oven," Walter said.

"I don't see no smoke from the chimney or a lantern light in the window," Sweetwater said.

"I don't, either," Walter said.

"Maybe they're still doing those chores you left them?"

"Soon to be dark with no fire going," Walter said. He passed Sweetwater the reins to the mule. "Take the mule, Sweet. I'm going to find out."

Walter tapped his spurs and yanked the reins and the powerful horse raced across the range to the cabin. Walter jumped from the saddle and ran up the steps into the cabin. It was deserted and cold. He opened the woodstove door. The last fire was at least twelve hours ago from this morning. There were no dirty pans or plates, nothing to show they had breakfast.

As Walter stepped back outside to the porch, Sweetwater arrived with the mule.

"Last fire was this morning," Walter said. "And they had no breakfast."

Sweetwater dismounted. "Check out back?"

"Not yet."

Walter and Sweetwater walked around the side of the cabin where they spotted Slicker on the ground beside the outhouse. They ran to him. He was on his stomach. His legs and hands were tied with rope. A red checkered bandana was in his mouth and tied behind his head to keep him from calling out. There was no need for the bandana. Slicker was badly beaten and unconscious.

"Let's get him in the cabin," Walter said as he cut the ropes with his knife.

Together, they lifted Slicker and carried him inside and set him on a bed.

Walter washed and attended to the many cuts and bruises on

Slicker's face while Sweetwater boiled a pot of coffee and made some food at the oven.

"Looks like they weren't happy just beating him, they put the boots to him as well," Walter said as he went to the table.

Sweetwater brought two cups of coffee to the table. "Slick was never one to go lightly," he said.

"Whatever happened here, maybe the boy ran for cover?" Walter said.

"Maybe."

"Ain't likely though, is it?"

"No." Sweetwater sipped coffee, then turned to look at Slicker. "Is he going to wake up?"

"Maybe not till morning," Walter said. "He's had a rough go. We'll have to take turns watching him through the night."

"You think it was Indians?" Sweetwater said.

"Indians don't steal thirteen-year-old boys for no reason and they certainly don't leave men alive roped up like cattle," Walter said. "They'd a just killed him and be done with it. We'll just have to wait for Slick to wake up and tell us what happened."

Walter was asleep in a chair at the table when a loud moan from Slicker woke him up. He went to the bunk and found Slicker was slowly coming around. Walter lit two lanterns at the table and filled a cup with water.

"Slick, can you hear me?" Walter said.

Slicker opened his eyes and they glazed over. "Walt, is that you?"

"It is and Sweet," Walter said. "He's here, too."

Their voices woke Sweetwater and he got off his bunk. "He's awake."

"We got to sit him up," Walter said. "In a chair."

Walter and Sweetwater lifted Slicker into a chair at the table.

"Take a sip of water, but just a sip," Walter said.

Slicker took a small sip from the cup and set it aside. "My eyes ain't working so good," he said. "I see two of everything. Help me back to the bunk."

"No," Walter said. "Remember that time Sweet got kicked in the head roping a cow and was out for several days. The doc said he had what they call a concussion. He said it was vital to keep Sweet awake once he woke up. That's what I think you have, a concussion of the head."

Slicker nodded and took another sip of water. "Dammit, Walter, I was in the outhouse," he said. "The boy made a fire in the woodstove. We done all those chores you left us to do. I showed him how to rope and . . ."

"That's not important now," Walter said. "Tell us what happened. You were in the outhouse. Then what?"

"The door opened and a man with his face covered by a bandana pointed a gun at me," Slicker said. "Behind him were two more men, also with their faces covered. I figured they weren't going to shoot me or they would've already done so through the door, so I made a play. I got in a few licks before they pistol-whipped me. One of them kicked me when I was down and the next thing I know, I'm waking up in my bunk."

"Did they say anything?" Walter said.

"I heard one of them say saddle the boy's horse," Slicker said. "After that I was out cold until you found me."

"This ain't no robbery," Sweetwater said. "They took nothing but the boy."

"That's exactly what it is, a robbery," Walter said. "And the treasure they're after is in that boy."

"I don't understand, Walter," Sweetwater said. "What treasure?"

"My sister left the boy an inheritance," Walter said. "Enough to buy ten ranches, maybe more. Almost three hundred thousand dollars in cash alone."

"Who knows about this, Walter?" Slicker said.

"Them bankers and lawyers in New York," Walter said. "The boy's stepfather, although he stands to make a small fortune from the house my sister left him. And I hate to say it, the boy's family in California."

"Well, who's got the stomach for it?" Slicker said.

"It's amazing what you can stomach when a fortune is involved," Walter said. "Sweet, first light, ride out and pick up their trail while I pack supplies. Then you stay behind with Slick here and make sure he gets better. The boy will slow them down enough for me to catch them inside of two days."

"And do what?" Sweetwater said.

"I'm going to kill them," Walter said. "What do you think I'm gonna do?"

CHAPTER THIRTY-ONE

Walter was saddling his horse in the corral when Sweetwater rode in from his scouting. Sweetwater dismounted at the corral gate. "They rode south and from the looks of things, they're in no big hurry."

"Why should they be?" Walter said. "They got what they came for and don't think they're being followed. That's to my advantage."

"Our advantage," Sweetwater said.

"I told you, Sweet, you have to stay behind and see after Slick," Walter said.

"I can't stay behind and see after Slick, on account he ain't staying behind," Sweetwater said.

"What are you babbling about?" Walter said.

"Me," Slicker said from the porch. Dressed in black trail clothes, Slicker wore his Colt Peacemaker on his hip and carried the Henry rifle in his arms. He stepped down off the porch and walked to the corral.

"What do you think you're doing?" Walter said.

"I told him," Sweetwater said. "He won't listen."

"No man pistol-whips me and ties me like a hog," Slicker said. "Besides, the boy was in my care and I lost him. It's only right I should help get him back."

"Are you fit?" Walter said.

"Fit enough," Slicker said.

"Then saddle your horse while I gather more supplies," Walter said.

They rode hard, past noon and close to sundown. The final mile, they walked to allow the horses to cool down and avoid getting sick from a dead-stop run.

"Less than an hour of light, Walter," Slicker said. "We need to make camp."

"Up ahead there," Walter said. "Should be fresh water."

They walked another quarter mile, following the four sets of tracks. William had slowed them down considerably and Walter was starting to think it was deliberate. Crossing Colorado into Wyoming, the boy rode his mare with enough gate to keep pace with Walter's much larger horse. He was riding now at a third the pace and that was slowing the three men down to practically a crawl.

"You showed the boy to ride on a tall horse like I asked?" Walter said to Slicker.

"Took to it right off," Slicker said. "By his tracks, you'd think the boy was riding a mule deer and dragging a sled full of rocks."

"I suspect the boy is slowing him down for us to follow," Walter said.

They reached a narrow, shallow stream that ran down from the mountains forty miles away. They found four sets of tracks and a burned-out campfire.

"They camped here the first night," Sweetwater said as he examined the tracks.

"The boy is slowing them down all right," Slicker said. "They should be twenty, thirty miles more ahead by now. We're making ground, but not enough."

"Sweet, ride out a bit and pick up the tracks for the morning," Walter said. "Slick and I will make camp and get a fire going."

Sweetwater rode his horse across the narrow stream and picked up four sets of tracks on the other side. They were continuing to travel south. The boy's mare was taking half steps, preventing them from making any good time. He rode out a bit more and saw the four horses were keeping to a southwest path. He noted the trail, turned and rode back across the stream to camp.

Walter was brushing the mustang and Slicker was building a fire when Sweetwater arrived and dismounted.

"They headed southwest for sure," Sweetwater said.

"My guess is Denver and the railroad," Walter said.

"Well, that don't make no sense," Slicker said. "They could have headed east to Cheyenne and got the railroad there."

"The railroad in Cheyenne only goes east and west," Walter said. "They want to go south."

"To where?" Sweetwater said.

"Mexico," Walter said. "That's enough talk. Sweet, tend to your horse. Slick, get some grub going. We need to be up and out before sunrise."

After a quick supper, Walter rolled a cigarette around the campfire as he, Slicker and Sweetwater drank coffee from tin mugs.

"I don't understand something, Walter," Sweetwater said. "Say somebody did know about the boy's fortune, how does stealing him profit them?"

Walter struck a match and lit his cigarette. "Remember the range war we hired on for back in seventy-seven?" he said. "Those with the water rights fighting with the cattle barons over the land."

"I remember," Sweetwater said. "We was there, too, ya know."

"Then you remember some of them cattle barons hired that gang of cutthroats out of Utah to steal some children belonging to those with the water rights," Walter said. "We rescued what, five or six kids? They call that kidnapping and the object is to hold them kids for a ransom to get what they want. I believe they took William and plan to hold him for ransom money down in Mexico. Maybe they plan to contact his kin in California or his stepfather in New York to arrange payment, but one thing is for sure, they will kill the boy once payment is made."

"To who?" Slicker said. "Who is behind all this, Walt?"

"I'll be sure to ask him who he is right before I put a .45 bullet right between his eyes," Walter said.

Slicker stirred the fire with a stick.

Sweetwater stared at Walter as he sipped coffee.

"You best get it right in your head that I plan to murder every last one of them in cold blood if I have to," Walter said. "If you can't stomach that fact, ride out in the morning and if I live through this, I'll meet you at the line shack with the boy."

Slicker tossed the stick into the fire. "You got no call to speak to me or Sweet that way," he said. "We have backed your play, ate crap for grub and slept on the ground more often than not for twenty-five years. If you don't know we're with you, then you go straight to hell, Walter Burke."

Walter puffed on his cigarette. "I was out of line."

"You were," Slicker said.

"Thing is, I want you to understand I aim to kill every last one of them even if they surrender the boy unharmed," Walter said.

"That's murder, Walt," Sweetwater said.

"It is," Walter said. "Best get your mind around it if you're going to see this through with me."

"Maybe it won't come to that," Slicker said.

"Suit yourself," Walter said, tossed the cigarette into the fire and laid back on his bedroll. "But, I will do what I have to do to save the boy and make sure he has a future."

Chapter Thirty-Two

At first light, Sweetwater, the best tracker of the three, rode out to scout the trail left by the kidnappers. He rode past the point he reached last night and followed the tracks for another mile or more.

At camp, Walter and Slicker drank coffee and rolled cigarettes as they waited for Sweetwater to return. They had bacon sizzling in a pan and biscuits wrapped in brown paper they would warm up upon Sweetwater's return.

"What you said last night about murder, did you mean that?" Slicker said as he puffed on his cigarette.

"I did," Walter said.

Slicker sighed openly. "I've known and rode with you since sixty and we done some hard things together, Walt. But, no matter how hard, you always been fair. It's not like you to talk about outright murder. It makes us no better than the scum we been bringing in all these years."

"Maybe so, but that's my intention," Walter said. "I failed my sister twice in my lifetime. Once when I sent her to New York when she was the only kin I had and the second time when I wasn't there when she died. She entrusted me with the boy's safety and it's my own foolishness he's in this situation. If I had stayed on the train, we'd be in San Francisco by now and the boy's life wouldn't be in danger. I'll not fail my sister three times, no sir. I'll put every damn one of them in their grave before I allow that to happen."

"I understand how you feel, Walt," Slicker said. "And when the shooting starts, me and Sweet will be by your side. But, when the shooting's over and any of them is still alive, they stay alive for the law to have. That's the way it has to be, or me and Sweet pull out this very morning."

"If that's how you feel, that's how you feel," Walter said. "Turn around and head back, I'll go on by myself."

"I don't understand you, Walt," Slicker said. "I just don't understand."

"Folks that would steal a boy for his money won't stop because they failed once," Walter said. "You have to stop it from happening again and the only way to do that is to make the punishment severe enough that nobody will risk it a second time. You have rats on a ship, you don't kill one, you kill them all. I fear if I leave any alive they will try again in the future in California."

"We ain't talking about rats, Walter," Slicker said.

A look washed over Walter's face that sent a chill down Slicker's back. "Don't you cross me on this, Slick," Walter said. "You and Sweet best turn around while we're still friends with good intentions."

Before Slicker could respond, Sweetwater rode into camp hard and dismounted by the fire. "Tracks go out for a mile or more, Walt," Sweetwater said. "Then they ditched the boy's horse and he rode with one of the three men. They must have figured they would make better time that way."

"The boy's horse throw a shoe?" Walter said.

"No," Sweetwater said. "She ran off on her own east."

"She hurt?"

"No," Sweetwater said. "Her tracks are nice and even."

Walter said as he stood up. "I'll see you sometime back at the line shack."

Walter walked to his saddled horse and mounted up. Without

looking back, he rode off at a full run across the stream.

"What's going on, Slick?" Sweetwater said. "What's he mean back at the line shack?"

"He's got it in his head to kill them kidnappers even if he gets the boy back and some of them are still alive," Slicker said. "To discourage others from doing the same. He said he owed his sister that much."

"So you gonna let him ride out and take on the whole bunch by himself?" Sweetwater said.

"He don't give a man a choice," Slicker said. "Besides, I ain't gonna try to stop him, not when he's in one of his moods."

"And what happens to our ranch if Walt gets himself killed?" Sweetwater said. "Did we work all these years to just throw it away just when we're about to get it?"

"Well, what do you want me to do?" Slicker said. "He's a stubborn a man as ever born and you know that."

"It seems to me the only way to save Walt from himself is to go with him," Sweetwater said.

Slicker stared at Sweetwater. "Ah, hell, I know that," he said and reached for the coffee pot to fill his cup. "Sit and have a cup and we'll let him stew for a bit in his own juice."

Walter picked up the point where the boy ditched his mare and rode with one of the kidnappers. Like Sweetwater said, the mare rode east, but was nowhere to be seen. The added weight of the boy made a deeper print in the dirt and grass, but they made faster time without the boy's mare holding them back.

Walter slowed the mustang to a trot and kept following the trail left behind by the kidnappers. If he ate in the saddle and rode through sundown, he could reach Denver after dark. It occurred to him that he didn't know the schedule for the trains and that William could be on a train headed south this very moment. If they made it to Mexico, the boy was as good as dead.

Walter yanked the mustang to an abrupt stop. Something happened here, he observed as he dismounted. They stopped for a few minutes. He inspected the grass and dirt to see why.

The boy either jumped or fell from the horse he was doubled up on. One man, probably the one William was forced to ride with, dismounted to deal with the boy. Then they rode on, hopefully with the boy unharmed.

While Walter was still on one knee, he spotted Slicker and Sweetwater riding hard toward him. He stood up and waited for them to arrive.

"Boy fell off the horse," Walter said when they arrived.

"No sign of a struggle," Sweetwater said as he scanned the ground.

"No," Walter said.

"Let's go if we're going," Slicker said.

Walter mounted and they moved out at a trot.

"We can make Denver by tonight if we eat in the saddle and don't run the horses to a sweat," Walter said.

"And if they ain't there, we have to livery the horses or we'll have three dead animals," Slicker said.

"Tell me something I don't know," Walter said.

They rode another five miles and paused when the tracks indicated William fell from the horse a second time.

"You think the boy's trying to run away?" Slicker asked.

Walter scanned the area. "No sign he's trying to run."

"I don't understand then," Slicker said. "I know he can ride better than this."

Walter dismounted and knelt beside the tracks. "Sweet, get down here."

Sweetwater dismounted and knelt beside Walter.

"What's this look like to you?" Walter said.

Sweetwater looked at the bent grass and flat impressions. "Like the boy laid down to take a nap," he said.

Walter suddenly grinned. "The boy has asthma," he said. "He's faking attacks to slow them down the only way he can, by falling off the horse."

"Faking it," Slicker said with a laugh. "Some of you did rub off on him after all."

"Let's go before the boy falls all the way to Mexico," Walter said.

CHAPTER THIRTY-THREE

From a quarter mile distance, Denver lit up the night sky in a sort of eerie glow on the otherwise black horizon.

Walter stopped his horse and Slicker and Sweetwater pulled up beside him. Walter withdrew his Colt Peacemaker from the holster and checked his ammunition. Normally, he kept one chamber of the six empty to prevent an accidental discharge. He removed a .45-caliber bullet from his holster and filled the empty chamber.

"We ain't going in to shoot the place up, Walt," Slicker said. "This is Denver, not Dodge City."

"Maybe so, but I want to be prepared and I suggest you do the same," Walter said and withdrew the Winchester rifle from its saddle holster to check the load.

Slicker and Sweetwater did a quick check of their weapons, then they moved on toward Denver. As they rode closer, faint tones of piano music reached them.

When they reached the fringe of the city, Walter led them down a dark alley to the livery stables where they dismounted. The livery and office were dark.

"Damned place is never open," Walter said and banged on the office door.

"Most people don't check their horses in the middle of the night," Slicker said.

Walter banged on the door again. "Come on, old timer, I know you're in there."

A lantern lit in the window and the man inside peered out. He went to the office door, opened it and held the lantern close to Walter's face. "You again," the man said. "Don't you never sleep?"

"We got three animals here need tending," Walter said.

"Of course you do. Go on," the man said and closed the office door.

A moment later, the livery doors slid open and the man said, "Well, bring them in if you're staying."

Walter walked in without his horse. "I got fifty dollars in cash for you if you can answer a question," he said.

"Mister, I just run the livery," the man said.

"If you intend to keep running the livery, and breathing for that matter, you'll answer my question," Walter said and pulled his Colt Peacemaker.

"Walter, put that away," Slicker said as he stepped between Walter and the man. "What the hell's wrong with you, anyway? Go on, put it away."

Walter holstered the Colt, turned around and took his horse from Sweetwater.

"Three men kidnapped my friend's nephew," Slicker told the livery man. "They rode in here sometime today with the boy doubled up on one of their horses. Have you seen them is what my rude friend wants to know?"

The livery man rubbed his chin and looked at Walter. "Stole his kin, you say?"

"Boy of about thirteen," Walter said. "Thin, pale, looks like a good wind would blow him over."

The livery man nodded. "They were here late this afternoon," he said. "They sold their horses. I got them out back."

"Sold their horses?" Walter said. "They buy new ones?"

"No, sir," the livery man said. "I heard them talking about catching the ten o'clock train tomorrow morning."

"You mean, they're still in town?" Walter said.

"No trains tonight and they didn't buy new horses," the livery man said. "Unless they went for a very long walk, yes."

"And they left here with the boy?" Walter said.

"Sure did."

"What they look like?" Walter said.

"Big men, hard-looking. Wore Smith and Wesson .44's," the livery man said. "Dressed like eastern dudes. They had the look of professional men, if you know what I mean."

Walter counted out sixty dollars. "Ten for the horses, fifty to keep your mouth shut," he said.

Walter, Slicker and Sweetwater took their rifles and left the livery and stood in the dark on a side street.

"Now what?" Slicker said. "There must be two dozen saloons and half that many hotels in town, not to mention the boarding-houses. You want to check them all?"

"You got a better idea?" Walter said. "Maybe you'd like to stand here in the street and wait for them to come to us."

"Yeah, I got a better idea. Let's wake up Marshal Landon and see if he's spotted those three," Slicker said.

"You picked a good time to start thinking, Slick," Walter said.

"Somebody has to," Slicker said. "You sure ain't."

Sweetwater chuckled at that and Walter silenced him with a glare.

"Quit your cackling and let's go," Walter said.

They walked down Main Street to the center of town to the marshal's office. A light from inside showed through the window.

"Well, somebody's awake," Walter said as he opened the door.

A puppy-faced deputy sheriff looked up from the book he was writing in when Walter, Slicker and Sweetwater entered the office.

"Who are you?" Walter said.

"Deputy Sheriff Freed, sir. Marshal Landon was called out of town and the Sheriff's Office watches things in his absence," Freed said.

"Where's the sheriff?" Walter said.

"Across the street in his office," Freed said. "He's asleep and doesn't like to be disturbed unless it's an emergency."

"What's his name?" Walter said.

"The sheriff?" Freed said.

"Look here, Sweet, we found your lost brother," Walter said. "Yes, the sheriff, you stupid pipsqueak. What's his name?"

"Sheriff Freed doesn't like to be disturbed once he's gone to sleep," Freed said. "And I resent calling me a pipsqueak."

"Is that so?" Walter said. "Well, you tell your pa . . . never mind, we'll tell him ourselves."

Walter turned and stormed out of the office.

Sweetwater looked at Slicker. "What'd he mean by my lost brother, Slick?"

"Forget it, Sweet," Slicker said. "Let's go before he winds up in jail."

Slicker, Sweetwater and Deputy Freed rushed out to catch Walter, who was across the street and about to knock on the sheriff's door.

"Sheriff Freed, I'm here on official business," Walter said as he knocked on the door with the butt of the Winchester. "Wake up before I . . ."

Deputy Freed rushed past Slicker and Sweetwater. "My pa . . . I mean, the sheriff, don't like to be . . ."

The door opened, cutting Deputy Freed short.

A double-barrel shotgun poked through the dark opening. "Before you what?" Sheriff Freed said.

"No call for that, Sheriff," Walter said.

Sheriff Freed, a slightly overweight man in his fifties, said, "I'll decide what's called for. Now suppose you tell me why I ain't in my bed sleeping."

"I told them, Pa, but they wouldn't listen," Deputy Freed said.

"Shut up, Newton," Sheriff Freed snapped at his son. He looked at Walter. "Now what official business are you talking about?"

"Best make a pot of coffee, Sheriff," Walter said. "This will take a while."

Sheriff Freed glared at his son. "Well, go on, boil a pot."

Twenty minutes later, Sheriff Freed sat behind his desk, sipped coffee and said, "I believe kidnapping is a federal complaint."

"We ain't got time to wait for the marshal," Walter said. "I'm not sure if the boy is faking his asthma or not, but I don't want to take that chance."

"I'm not suggesting you wait," Sheriff Freed said. "But there's twenty or more saloons and a dozen hotels and half that many boardinghouses to search. We could be at it all night and not find the boy."

"Pa?" Deputy Freed said.

"Not now, Newton," Sheriff Freed said.

"If we split up, maybe we can cover . . ." Walter said.

"But, Pa," Deputy Freed said.

"For God's sake, boy, what is it?" Sheriff Freed snapped.

"I know where those three men are," Deputy Freed said.

"Haven't I told you never to hold back vital information?" Sheriff Freed said.

"I wasn't . . . I mean . . ." Deputy Freed said.

"Never mind that, where are they?" Sheriff Freed said.

CHAPTER THIRTY-FOUR

The Lucky Dollar Saloon and Gambling House was the largest establishment of its kind in Denver. With brass railings, wall-to-wall mirrors behind the bar, gaming tables from back east and a first-class call girl operation on the second floor, it was the finest and busiest gentleman's house in the state. Loud piano music reached the street, although there was no piano player. The piano was a windup scroll player from Boston, although also fully functional by keyboard if someone wanted to play it manually. No one in the Lucky Dollar did.

Walter peered through the plate-glass window from the dark plank wood sidewalk. "I see three dudes at a table sipping rye whiskey," he said.

Sheriff Freed looked at his son. "Is that them, Newton? Take a good look."

Deputy Freed stood beside Walter and peered through the window. "That's them. I don't see the boy, though."

"You sure?" Sheriff Freed said. "There must be two hundred men in there."

"I'm sure, Pa. I mean, Sheriff," Deputy Freed said. "I remember their faces and the dude clothes from when I saw them with the boy on the street."

Sheriff Freed turned to Walter, Slicker and Sweetwater. "You men wait out here," he said. "Newton and I will go in and speak with them quietly."

"They're armed, Pa," Deputy Freed said.

"Everybody in the damn saloon is armed, boy," Sheriff Freed said.

"What if they make a move?" Deputy Freed said.

"Then you back my play."

"We should have shotguns, Pa."

Walter stepped past Sheriff Freed and shoved open the swinging doors, aimed his Winchester at the roof and fired a shot. The confined blast was loud and brought the entire saloon to a dead stop, except for the automatic piano.

Walter cocked the lever and fired a second shot into the piano, silencing it. "I got everybody's attention now!" Walter yelled.

Slicker, Sweetwater, Sheriff Freed and Deputy Freed filed in behind Walter.

"No call for that," Sheriff Freed said.

"Maybe so, but I could die of old age waiting for you and your boy to shut up, or make a decision," Walter said.

"This is an official call of business," Sheriff Freed said. "Everybody stay as you are in your seats."

The bartender came around the bar and walked to Sheriff Freed. "This lunatic shot a hole in my roof, and my piano, Sheriff. I want to . . ."

Walter whacked the bartender in the nose with the butt of his Winchester. The bartender fell to the floor as if shot.

"The man said nobody move," Walter said. "Don't you hear so good?"

Sheriff Freed turned to Slicker and Sweetwater. "Can you control him?"

"Knock it off, Walt," Slicker said. "Let the man do his job."

"Well, go ahead and do it if you're doing it," Walter said. "I ain't stopping you."

Sheriff Freed walked to the table where the three men his son pointed out sat and watched. They were dressed eastern style, clean-shaven, big, hard-looking men. They eyed Freed without fear but with respect, for despite his non-threatening appearance, they could see Freed was a man who could take charge when need be.

"Pistols on the table, belly guns, too," Sheriff Freed said.

The three men slowly removed massive .44 Schofield pistols from their holsters and set them on the table, then removed .32 pocket guns from their belts and set them beside the Schofields.

"Now we will adjourn to my office for some quiet conversation," Sheriff Freed said. "Newton, get their guns."

CHAPTER THIRTY-FIVE

Walter, Slicker and Sweetwater stood in the background and sipped coffee from tin cups while the three men stood before Sheriff Freed, who sat behind his desk. Deputy Freed stood to the left of the Sheriff with a shotgun cradled in his arms.

"Now suppose we start with names and identification if any is available," Sheriff Freed said.

"Thomas Dodge," one of them said.

"Wallace Winslow," another said.

"Albert Bell," the third said.

"I assume you can prove you are who you say," Sheriff Freed said.

Dodge, Winslow and Bell produced flap leather wallets and set them on the desk. Sheriff Freed picked up a wallet and opened it to reveal a Pinkerton's detective badge, along with identification for Thomas Dodge, agent for the famous agency.

"All of you?" Sheriff Freed said.

Dodge nodded his head.

Sheriff Freed held the wallet up for Walter, Slicker and Sweetwater to see.

"Pinkerton detectives?" Walter said. "You three? What the hell do you want with my nephew?"

"I'll ask the questions," Sheriff Freed said. "And that was a good one. How about it you three, why did you take the boy?"

"Our employer contacted the office in Philadelphia when you left the train with the boy in Dodge City," Winslow said. "It was assumed the boy had been kidnapped."

"He was kidnapped," Walter said. "By you three monkeys."

"How did you men get involved?" Freed asked.

"We were finishing up another assignment in Dodge when our office contacted us about the missing boy," Winslow said. "Our client hired the firm to find him. We picked up your trail in Dodge and tracked you to the line shack."

"You were supposed to take the boy to San Francisco to live with his mother's family by her first marriage," Bell said to Walter.

"I was taking him, you big dandy," Walter said. "By horse, from Laramie to San Francisco. I left the boy with my partner, the one you pistol-whipped, to buy a mule and supplies for the trip. I wanted the boy to see some open country and learn a few things about life and horses before he started private school."

"You pistol-whipped a man?" Sheriff Freed said. He looked at Slicker's face. "Him?"

"We thought he was a kidnapper," Dodge said.

"You thought wrong," Walter said.

"Where is the boy now?" Sheriff Freed said.

"It's against our company policy to reveal the identity of a client once we've been engaged by them," Dodge said. "I'm sorry."

Walter smacked Dodge in the face with the stock of his Winchester and Dodge fell to his knees with blood streaming from his nose. "Is it your company policy to get a boy killed?" Walter said. "You horse's ass."

"That will be enough of that," Sheriff Freed said.

Dodge slowly stood up and held his nose. "We didn't know, Sheriff. We just follow orders from the home office."

"Maybe so, but this is one time you will break those orders or stand in my jail until the federal marshal returns from up north and you answer to kidnapping and assault charges,"

Sheriff Freed said.

Dodge looked at Bell and Winslow. They nodded yes.

"Our Philadelphia office was hired to find the boy once you left the train with him," Dodge said. "Our client is out of New York. Jordan Beal, the boy's stepfather. He claimed he didn't trust you alone with the boy. He hired a man to stay on the train and keep watch over you two and when you got off, he wired Mr. Beal."

"I might have guessed it was that Beal behind this," Walter said.

"You know the man?" Sheriff Freed said.

"We met in New York," Walter said. "My sister didn't trust him and neither do I. He must have hired a man figuring to get the boy off the train at some point and stash him away."

"Why?" Sheriff Freed said.

"My sister was a wealthy woman," Walter said. "She left it all to the boy and nothing to Beal. I figure now that he has the boy, he'll want money to return him to his family."

"That's kidnapping and ransom," Sheriff Freed said. "I'll send a wire to Landon right away."

"To go where?" Walter said, looking at Dodge.

"I don't know," Dodge said. "Our contract was to deliver the boy to Mr. Beal, and we turned the boy over to him at the hotel as soon as we reached town. That was eight hours ago. They left town immediately."

"Was Beal alone?" Sheriff Freed said.

"Had eight men with him," Dodge said. "One of them was William Russel. I figure the others were his bunch."

"William Russel out of Missouri, who rents his gun out to settle landowner disputes and such?" Sheriff Freed said.

"I expect so," Dodge said.

"What the hell does Beal need protection from?" Sheriff Freed said.

Dodge looked at Walter. "My guess is him."

"They say where they were headed?" Sheriff Freed said.

"Not directly," Bell said. "I heard Russel say in the lobby of the hotel he didn't want to cross the Rio Grande in a boat and Beal said he would pay them extra for the trouble."

"Beal aims to hole up in Mexico until he gets his ransom money," Walter said. "I doubt he'll let the boy go alive once he's paid."

"Alamosa is where they would have to cross," Sheriff Freed said. "I could wire the marshal and form a posse."

"Denver to Alamosa is a hundred and fifty miles," Walter said. "If we left at sunup, they'd have a hundred-mile head start, more on the marshal and his posse. That's more ground to cover than Rhode Island is large."

"Maybe the agency has some men down at the border?" Dodge said. "Sheriff, is the telegraph office open?"

Sheriff Freed turned to his son. "Newton, take them to the telegraph office and have them open up for them."

"Right away, Pa," Deputy Freed said.

"We'll be in the saloon having a drink if you get word," Walter said. "And even if you don't."

CHAPTER THIRTY-SIX

Wearing a white bandage over his nose, the bartender set a bottle of rye and three glasses on the table and looked at Walter. "I've since heard about your boy from some of the men," he said. "And I'm sorry. I hope you get him back."

"Hold on a minute," Walter said. He dug out the roll of expense money and counted out five hundred dollars. "For the repair of the piano and your roof," Walter said and gave the bills to the bartender.

The bartender nodded as he looked at Walter. "You boys took the Smith brothers out of here a year ago," he said. "I should have recognized you."

"We'll call it even," Walter said. "If the five hundred ain't enough, have the marshal send me a wire."

The bartender nodded and returned to the bar.

Walter, Slicker and Sweetwater picked up their shots of rye and downed them in one quick gulp. Walter picked up the bottle and refilled the glasses.

Dodge, Bell and Wallace entered the saloon and approached the table. Dodge had a white bandage over his swollen nose. "We sent a wire to our office and another to Marshal Landon, for what that's worth," Dodge said.

"It's not worth a lot, but I appreciate the effort," Walter said. "Sit and have a drink with us. It's the least I can do for busting your nose."

Wallace went to the bar and returned with three glasses. He,

Dodge and Bell pulled up three chairs and Walter filled the glasses with rye.

"You have to believe our office would never have contracted with Beal had they knew what he was up to," Dodge said.

"And for what that's worth, I believe you," Walter said. "But Landon is north of here and come morning, Beal and his bunch will have a hundred miles or more head start on us."

"You plan to follow them?" Dodge said.

"Right into Mexico and straight to hell if I have to," Walter said.

"They'll hang you for murder in Mexico just because you're American," Dodge said. "And understand we aren't authorized to go with you or we would, at least to the border."

"I hold you not responsible for what that snake Jordan Beal did," Walter said.

Dodge lifted his shot of rye. "I hope you get the boy back safely," he said and he, Wallace and Bell downed their shots.

"Maybe we'll cross paths again sometime on a happier occasion," Walter said.

Dodge nodded, then he, Wallace and Bell left the saloon.

Slicker took a sip from his glass. "Mexico, Walter?" he said.

"I ain't asking you to go," Walter said. "That Dodge fellow is right. The Mexican government has no fond feelings for Americans, especially if they start shooting up the countryside."

"Aw, hell," Slicker said. "We'll go anywhere you go, Walt. I figure, it's my fault for losing the boy in the first place and Sweet feels as I do."

Slicker and Walter looked at Sweetwater, who was focused on his shot glass.

"What's the matter, Sweet?" Walter said. "Rye got your tongue?"

Sweetwater stood up. "I'll be back directly," he said, and rushed out of the saloon.

Slicker shrugged. "If he's going to the outhouse, he's going the wrong way."

Sweetwater crossed the street and entered the Sheriff's office. Sheriff Freed was behind his desk, writing in a book. He looked up at Sweetwater.

"You can tell your friend Burke, the marshal has been duly notified," Sheriff Freed said. "I was just making the official telegram entry in my log book."

"I'll tell him, but that ain't why I'm here," Sweetwater said. "I want to send some telegrams of my own, but I don't write so good. Can you send them for me?"

"What do you want to say?" Sheriff Freed said.

"Well, I have me an idea," Sweetwater said. "Maybe your boy won't mind taking a ride?"

CHAPTER THIRTY-SEVEN

Walter, Slicker and Sweetwater led three mustang horses out of the livery stables an hour before sunrise. Each horse was slim and in its prime, built for speed. They carried just a saddle and holster for a Winchester rifle and canteen to keep the weight low. Each rifle holster held a rifle.

Sheriff Freed, his son Newton and the stable manager stood by the open livery doors. "Any horses don't survive the ride, I'll pay for," Walter said.

Slicker mounted his mustang, as did Sweetwater.

"This is just crazy enough to work," Sheriff Freed said.

Walter mounted his mustang and looked at Sweetwater. "Sweet, you picked the right time to get the idea of your life," he said and dug his spurs into the sides of the horse.

With a powerful jerk, Walter rode off, closely followed by Slicker and Sweetwater.

"Them horses won't last ten miles at that pace," Deputy Freed said.

"That's the point, son," Sheriff Freed said.

"Killing good horses is the point?" Deputy Freed said.

"Those boys rode for the Pony Express," Sheriff Freed said. "They're express riders."

"They'll never catch them," the stable manager said.

"They'll catch them," Sheriff Freed said. "Or die trying."

★　★　★　★　★

They rode in flank formation with less than a yard separating the horses and covered the first mile out of town in less than two minutes. After the second mile, steam rose from the horses' flared nostrils. By the fifth mile, the horses started to sweat a white lathery sheen.

By the seventh mile, the lathery sheen was a thick foamy coat of sweat that flew off their chests and haunches in salty, soapy clumps.

Steam rose off the horses' shoulders and from their nostrils.

Walter knew the signs from his days at the Pony Express. Another three miles and the horses would enter the danger zone from overheating. They would start to cramp and if you stopped and let them drink before they cooled down, they would get sick and possibly die.

Slicker glanced over at Sweetwater. "They gonna be there!" he shouted above the thundering noise of the horses' hooves.

"They'll be there!" Sweetwater shouted.

Mark Peyton and his wife Emily started their ranch in sixty-three at the height of the war. They weren't barons by any stretch, but they made out all right and even put some money away for their old age. And in the twenty-two years they've been ranchers, they'd seen many things. Range wars over grazing and water rights, the railroad connecting the country, Denver growing from a small town to a major metropolis, the telegraph and soon, to hear tell it, the telephone.

Never had the Peytons heard of anything they were about to witness. As Deputy Freed instructed, they stood on the range with their three fastest horses, saddled and ready to go just before dawn.

The sun slowly rose over the horizon. The tall grass of the open range appeared a dull orange for a few minutes until the sun was high enough in the sky and then they were in a sea of emerald green.

"Do you see anything?" Emily said as she squinted into the sun.

"Not yet . . . wait, I see something," Mark said.

"Where?"

"There, directly ahead," Mark said. "And coming fast."

Emily cupped her hands over her eyes and squinted. "I see them."

Mark and Emily stood and watched as the three horses raced across the range toward them. When the horses were near enough, they could see the thick clumps of foam fly off their backs and steam rise from their nostrils.

It seemed the very ground shook when the horses arrived. The three men in the saddles grabbed their Winchester rifles and canteens and jumped to the ground. Immediately, they ran to the fresh horses.

"Appreciate the loan of the horses," one of the men said as they mounted the fresh horses. "I'll pay for any injuries to yours on the ride."

"Don't water those three for at least half an hour," another of the three men said.

"I'll take care of them," Mark said, and then the three men rode off at a furious pace. "When they're rested, I'll return them to the livery."

Inside of a minute, they were a quarter mile away. Mark turned to Amy. "Ain't this the damndest thing you ever saw," he said.

The rancher's horses weren't the caliber of those from the livery in town, but they were powerful and knew the terrain, which was a definite benefit. A horse used to a certain terrain isn't skittish about falling in a hole or tripping and breaking a leg, so they were able to run these three flat out.

Slicker had a slight lead on Walter and Sweetwater, being the lightest of the three and the best rider. "Hey, Walter!" Slicker shouted above the thunder of horse hooves. "Like the old days, ain't it?"

"Ain't nothing like the old days!" Walter shouted. "Nothing we will ever do will be like the old days!"

"Because of progress?" Slicker shouted.

"Because we was young!" Walter shouted and dug his spurs into the horse and raced ahead of Slicker.

By late afternoon, Walter, Slicker and Sweetwater changed horses six times. With each change, the crowd of people seeing them off grew larger. Walter didn't count, but there must have been fifty people gathered in a field to watch them change mounts.

A man changed out their canteens. A woman gave them biscuits and corn dodgers they could eat in the saddle. As they rode off, the gathered crowd let out with a loud cheer and applause.

As they rode into a large gathering of ranchers and farmers for the ninth change of horses, Walter, Slicker and Sweetwater paused for a moment to accept hot cups of coffee and warm biscuits.

A man stepped forward. "My name is Howard and these are my best three mounts," he said.

"We're obliged to you, Mr. Howard," Walter said. "I'll pay for any damages to your animals, don't worry."

"I'm not worried," Howard said. "I am concerned, however, that it will be dark shortly and you will be riding blind."

Walter looked at the sky. "We might make the next change if we hurry."

"And if you don't, you'll have to make a cold camp," Howard said.

"Mr. Howard has a point, Walter," Slicker said.

"Then you stay and discuss it with him," Walter said and climbed aboard his horse. "And I'll see you at the Grande."

With a kick, Walter was off and running.

"You best go with him, son," Howard said.

Slicker took a final sip of coffee and handed the cup to Howard. "Obliged," he said and he and Sweetwater mounted up and rode off after Walter.

A crowd of a hundred or more ranchers, farmers and citizens of Pueblo gathered in the open range to await the three cowboys. They set up picnic tables, had food cooking on fires and spits, and some even brought bedrolls. One man brought a banjo and was strumming a tune in the background.

The mood of the crowd was festive and loud. Then, as the sun went down, they fell silent. Within minutes of sunset, the prairie was blanketed in a moonless darkness.

"I can't see my hand in front of my face," a man said. "They'll never see us out there in the dark."

"Maybe we should send a few riders with torches to see if they can spot them?" another man said.

"And when our riders get lost?" a third man said. "Who goes out for them?"

"Damn, they'll never see us for sure," a fourth man said.

"Yes, they will," an older woman said. She picked up a stick and went to a picnic table where she wrapped a linen cloth around the stick. She picked up a jug of mash whiskey and doused the linen with it, then dipped the stick in a fire. The alcohol-soaked cloth immediately ignited.

"Some of you men grab sticks," the older woman said. "A lot of sticks."

Walter, Slicker and Sweetwater slowed their horses to a slow walk.

"Dammit, Walt, we can't see nothing," Slicker said. "Maybe if we had a full moon, but we don't. We have to stop and camp."

"How far you figure we come?" Walter said.

"Too far and not far enough," Slicker said. "I suggest we stop before we get turned around and lose our bearing for morning."

Walter stopped his horse, and Slicker and Sweetwater stopped beside him. "You may be right. What do you think, Sweet?"

"I think you should look at that before we decide," Sweetwater said, and pointed to a dozen or more lit torches in the distance.

Walter and Slicker looked at the torches. "That's not more than a half mile away," Slicker said.

"Well, we shouldn't keep our hosts waiting," Walter said.

They rode in easy and as they approached the large crowd, cheers broke out in celebration. A banjo played a welcoming tune. As they dismounted, dozens from the crowd surrounded them.

"We knew you'd make it," a man said.

"We got hot coffee and food," a woman said. "And we made some pies."

"Come by the fire," a man said. "Get these men some coffee."

Walter, Slicker and Sweetwater were whisked to the campfire where a dozen wood chairs were arranged in a circle.

"Sit," a man said. "Bring these men some food."

Walter, Slicker and Sweetwater took chairs. Cups of hot coffee were placed in their hands.

"I'm touched by this display," Walter said. "My name is . . ."

"We know who you are," the sheriff of Pueblo, Ned Jackson, said.

"I know you," Walter said. "You're the sheriff over at Pueblo. We brought some rustlers to your jail a few years back."

"The entire state is talking about this," Jackson said. "The last Pony Express ride, they're calling it. Even got some news-paper people writing about it, calling you boys express riders."

"They calling us what?" Slicker said.

"Express riders," Jackson said. "They plan a series of stories in the eastern newspapers."

"Well, I'll be," Slicker said.

"That's what all these folks are doing out here in the middle of nowhere in the dark," Walter said.

Two women brought three plates of food. "I hope you find that no-good bushwhacker who stole the boy and hang him from a tall tree," one woman said.

"And leave him to rot," the second woman added.

"My sentiments exactly," Walter said.

"We'll fill your coffee cups," the other woman said.

"A man could get spoiled from all this fuss," Walter said.

"Is that apple pie I'm smelling?" Sweetwater said.

"Yes, it is," the first woman said. "We baked it special just for you."

"Bring me a coffee and then let me talk to these men alone for a while," Jackson said.

The women returned to a table. One woman brought Jackson a cup. "There you go, Sheriff," she said and went back to the table.

Jackson took a sip from the cup. "How many miles you figure you three rode today?" he said.

"Hundred ten, maybe hundred fifteen," Slicker said.

"You figure to catch them tomorrow nightfall?" Jackson said.

"We're riding three times the miles they are," Walter said. "If not nightfall tomorrow, the first thing the day after, but we'll catch them, that's for sure."

"I understand William Russel is leading the bunch," Jackson said.

"The boy's stepfather is paying the freight, but Russel is the man in charge is my guess," Walter said. "You know him?"

"We crossed paths," Jackson said. "He's faster than most and deadly accurate and from what I've seen he enjoys his work a great deal."

"What are you saying?" Slicker said.

"It might be wise to wait for the marshal and his posse," Jackson said.

"That might be the wise thing to do, but if they cross into Mexico, I'll never see the boy alive," Walter said.

"I understand," Jackson said. "If it were my kin, I'd do the same thing. Well, I have to get back to town. I'll see you off in the morning."

After things quieted down and most of the ranchers, farmers and townsfolk returned home, Walter, Slicker and Sweetwater spread the bedrolls by the fire and settled in under blankets.

Walter rolled a cigarette and struck a match. "Fine bunch of folks they have in these parts," Walter said. "We could do worse starting our ranch in this country."

Somewhere in the dark, a horse snorted.

"My back is killing me," Sweetwater said. "Feels like I been kicked by a mule."

"We all feel that way, Sweet," Slicker said. "We ain't kids no more."

"Think how them horses must feel," Walter said.

"Walt?" Slicker said. "This Russel must be pretty good to hire his gun out the way he does."

"I never had the pleasure of meeting the man," Walter said.

"But, any man hires his gun out is a man to be feared."

"I ain't talking about fear," Slicker said. "I'm thinking this Beal must want the boy's money real bad to hire the likes of Russel and his bunch to do his dirty work."

"Beal is one of those men who always says the right thing, but you always have the feeling he never means a word he says," Walter said.

"Like a politician," Sweetwater said.

"That profession does come to mind," Walter said.

"Even if he manages to get to Mexico and get his hands on the boy's money, he won't let the boy go," Slicker said. "He might not kill the boy outright, but he'll sure as hell just leave him there stranded to fend for himself."

"I know it," Walter said.

"The boy won't have a chance alone in the Mexican desert," Slicker said.

"I know that, too," Walter said.

"For what, more money?" Sweetwater said.

"Money is a funny thing, Sweet," Walter said. "The more you own of it, the more it seems to own you."

"Right now, the only thing I want to own is some sleep," Slicker said.

Chapter Thirty-Eight

"More coffee, boys?" a woman asked as she held a coffee pot.

"Just a touch," Walter said.

The crowd returned at dawn, not as large as last night, but they brought hot food and biscuits. Sheriff Jackson was with them and he had some news.

"I wired every lawman south to the Grande," Jackson said. "No one has seen Beal or the boy. Means they're camping on the range away from towns."

"Means Beal probably hasn't got the word on us coming," Walter said.

"That would be my guess," Jackson said.

Walter rolled a cigarette and struck a wood match. "If we get close to Beal late today, I want all the farmers and ranchers to stay home," he said. "If we have to tangle with them on the open range, things will get ugly and I don't want no innocent folks getting hurt or killed."

"Maybe I can send some wires today and have some posses out scouting for them?" Jackson said.

"Obliged," Walter said. "Well, we best mount up before our bellies are so full we slow the horses down."

A rancher had three horses saddled and ready to go. "These are my three finest horses," he said.

"We'll do our best to keep them uninjured," Walter said.

Three changes of horses later, after forty miles of hard riding, they stopped for coffee, biscuits and bacon provided by a gathered crowd.

Four changes later, Sweetwater slowed to a stop and dismounted. Walter and Slicker stopped and stayed on their horses.

"What is it, Sweet?" Slicker said.

Sweetwater squatted down beside the tracks left behind by Beal and the group. "Turning west a bit," he said.

"West?" Walter said.

"Wait here," Sweetwater said, mounted his horse and rode out about a half mile, tracking the prints.

"Maybe they ran out of supplies and are looking for a town?" Slicker said.

"Ain't no town west of here for quite a ways," Walter said.

Sweetwater came racing back. "They definitely headed west," he said.

"How far ahead of us are they?" Walter said.

"No more than four hours," Sweetwater said.

"They're taking it easy," Walter said. "Going for supplies and in no hurry about it means they don't suspect we're this close. What do you want to do?"

"If we follow them, we won't have fresh horses for the morning," Slicker said. "And we have a cold camp without any supplies except water."

"Sweet?" Walter said.

"We could ride to the next change and pick up fresh horses, but by then it will be dark and we'll never find this turnoff until morning," Sweetwater said. "I say we go west and follow them."

"Same here," Slicker said.

"West it is, but we can't run these animals or they will be useless in the morning without grain," Walter said.

They rode until sundown and stopped on the open range where the horses had sweet grass to graze on.

"This is as far as we go tonight," Walter said. "We don't want to get turned around in the dark."

"Anybody got something to eat?" Slicker said as he dismounted.

"A few biscuits," Sweetwater said.

"Some jerky sticks," Walter said.

Sweetwater dismounted and peered in the distance. "What's that over there?" he said, and pointed.

Still mounted with a higher view, Walter looked where Slicker pointed and said, "Appears to be lights of some kind. I think its lanterns."

"Lanterns?" Slicker said. "There ain't no town west of here for ten or more miles at least."

"Maybe so, but we're looking at something," Walter said. "Build a fire to guide me back. I'm going for a look."

"Be careful, Walt," Slicker said. "That could be a trap."

"If it is, they're springing it from a quarter mile away," Walter said and rode off.

A hundred yards out, Walter could see the makings of a new town being built. The lantern lights came from windows of finished buildings. Most of the town was still in the planning and building stages.

Walter rode in slowly so as not to attract attention. The base of the town was a completed railroad depot, although there wasn't a track in sight in either direction. Those building the town completed the essentials first, a hotel, saloon, some shops, a livery stable, supply store. Everything else, another twenty structures, was in the planning process for future building. Wagons full of wood and building materials were everywhere.

On the main street into town, Walter dismounted. Behind the

town limits in an open field, he could see the faint outline of dozens of pitched tents with some fires going in front of them.

Walter walked his horse down the street to where he saw a lantern in the office window of the livery stable. He tied his horse to the post out front, then opened the office door and entered.

A man with snowy white hair and rimmed spectacles looked up from the books he was writing in and looked at Walter. His eyes told Walter the man was startled.

"Easy, mister," Walter said. "I mean you no harm. I got a horse outside could use some oats and two more on the range. I have money to pay for what I need."

"Ten pounds do?" the man said.

"Twenty, if you can spare it and maybe something for us as well," Walter said.

"If you have money, why don't you try the hotel?" the man said. "It's got right comfortable beds."

"Because I'm after nine men and a boy," Walter said. "I believe they headed to your town. Have you seen them?"

"Maybe you best tell me why you're after them?" the man said.

"The boy is my sister's son," Walter said. "She died and left the boy an inheritance of considerable worth. The man leading that bunch is the boy's stepfather and he kidnapped the boy and aims to steal the inheritance. The men riding with him are William Russel and his bunch. Russel is a hired gun hand and a damn good one at that from what I hear."

The man stared at Walter.

"At first light, me and my partners aim to get the boy back from his stepfather," Walter said. "And unless I mistake that no-good snake Jordan Beal for what he is, there will be considerable shooting in the process."

"Mister, this town ain't even built yet," the man said. "It's commissioned by the railroad and they own everything in it. The people building this town are good people. There isn't a gun hand in the bunch. Carpenters and women is what we got here."

"Most of them live in those tents?" Walter said.

"Except for the hotel staff and me," the man said. "And the saloon."

"Before first light, ride out to the tents and tell everyone to stay put, and that goes for you as well," Walter said.

"What's to stop them from riding out at first light?" the man said.

"For one thing, a man can't ride a horse he don't have," Walter said. "So when you ride out to see the townsfolk, you bring their horses with you."

"How do I know you ain't spinning one big tale on me?" the man said. "For your own gain."

"Gain of what?" Walter said. "To profit wood and nails at three-to-one odds?"

The man stared at Walter.

"The boy look pale and thin to you?" Walter said.

"He did."

"They plan to leave him in Mexico after they get his money," Walter said. "Even if they don't kill him outright, how long you think he'll survive on his own in the Mexican desert?"

The man slid open a desk drawer and produced a pint bottle of whiskey. "Have a drink while I get your supplies," he said.

Walter followed the campfire back to Slicker and Sweetwater. From a distance, he could smell roasting meat, which turned out to be rabbit on a spit made of sticks.

"That aroma has whet my appetite," Walter said as he dismounted.

"Sweet caught a rabbit," Slicker said. "Knocked it out with a rock. Damndest thing I ever saw."

"Maybe you should pitch for one of them eastern baseball teams," Walter said.

"What's baseball?" Sweetwater said.

"It's a game, you dumb river rat," Slicker said.

Walter removed the sack slung over his saddle and set it by the fire. "Man gave me a pot of baked beans, fresh bread and bacon, plates and coffee with pot and cups," he said. "And a bottle of this," he said and tossed the whiskey bottle to Slicker.

"A man gave you all this?" Slicker said.

"For the promise not to kill any innocent people," Walter said.

"Maybe you best tell us what happened in that town," Slicker said.

"Can we eat first?" Sweetwater said.

CHAPTER THIRTY-NINE

Walter rolled a cigarette and used a stick from the fire to light it. He opened the pint bottle of whiskey and poured an ounce into his coffee cup, then passed the bottle to Slicker, who did the same.

"We have enough coffee, bacon and bread for a quick breakfast in the morning," Walter said.

Slicker gave the bottle to Sweetwater, who added some to his coffee.

"Right fine whiskey," Slicker said.

"Livery man said the bottle was for luck," Walter said. "And I expect we can use some come sunup."

"Luck don't mean nothing when it's three-to-one odds," Slicker said.

"That's when it means it the most, so I want you to read and sign something for me," Walter said and produced a folded piece of paper from his shirt pocket. "The man was kind enough to give me pencil and paper."

"What's that?" Sweetwater asked.

"Read it and sign it," Walter said. "And give the paper to Slick."

Sweetwater moved closer to the fire for light and stared at the words on the page.

"Don't burn it up, Sweet," Walter said. "I got no more paper."

"What's it say?" Slicker said.

"In the . . . odor of . . ." Sweetwater said.

214

"What?" Slicker said. "Give me that," he said and snatched the paper from Sweetwater. "Odor, you dumb mule. That says order."

"Order of what?" Sweetwater said.

Slicker looked at Walter. "Of Walt's death," Slicker said. "If he gets killed and we survive, he wants us to take the boy to California."

"What if we all get killed?" Sweetwater said.

"Then it don't matter if you sign the damn paper or not," Walter said and flipped Slicker a pencil. "Now sign it or I go alone in the morning."

"No need to get in one of your moods," Slicker said and signed the paper.

Sweetwater took the paper and pencil. "What should I write?"

Slicker and Walter looked at each other and cracked up laughing.

"What?"

"Your name, Sweet," Slicker said. "Write your name."

"I know that," Sweetwater said. "I thought Walt might want some special words."

"Just your name is special enough," Walter said as he tossed the spent cigarette into the fire.

Sweetwater scribbled his name and returned the paper to Walter.

Walter rolled and lit another cigarette as he looked up at the stars. "It's a fine clear night," he said. "Perfect for sleeping."

"It would be if you'd be quiet," Slicker said.

"The odds are three to one against us," Walter said. "It ain't likely all of us will survive an outright shootout. We have to kill Beal first and maybe Russel and his men will quit without a payment coming."

"You know I can't hit nothing unless I got time to take careful aim," Sweetwater said.

"Ain't important in a firefight," Walter said. "Shoot fast and often, you'll hit something sooner or later."

"What if we kill Beal and Russel decides to keep the boy and cash in for himself?" Slicker said.

"Then we will kill them all, or they kill us," Walter said.

"Russel's that good, huh?" Slicker said.

"We've seen his kind many times before," Walter said. "Men like Russel are most dangerous when someone is shooting at them. Their blood gets up and you can see the lust for more blood in their eyes. Once they start, they don't stop until there's no one left to kill or you kill them."

"You're fine company tonight," Slicker said. "What are you trying to do, scare us like children with the boogey man?"

"No," Walter said. "I just want you to understand what we're riding into come morning. What's your thoughts, Sweet?"

"He fell asleep five minutes ago," Slicker said. "And if you don't mind, I'm joining him."

Slicker rolled over and faced the waning campfire.

Walter took a puff on the cigarette and stared up at the stars. "It's a fine beautiful night," he said.

CHAPTER FORTY

Walter took a sip of hot coffee, then bit into a cold biscuit. "Be light in about an hour," he said. "How's that bacon coming?"

Slicker stirred the bacon in the pan and added the remains of last night's beans. "About ten minutes," he said.

"There's a couple of snorts left in this bottle," Walter said, and emptied the whiskey into the frying pan. "We might as well have it with breakfast in case we ain't around for lunch."

"That ain't funny, Walter," Sweetwater said.

"Ain't trying to be funny," Walter said. "I just hate to waste good sipping whiskey if it could be put to good use."

"Rider coming," Slicker said.

As dawn started to break, the faint outline of a man on horseback riding toward them slowly materialized on the dark horizon.

"Let him come," Walter said.

"What if it's one of Russel's men?" Sweetwater said.

"They wouldn't send one man on a horse slower than a mule," Walter said.

Slicker lifted the pan off the fire. "Might as well eat while we wait for him," he said. "As slow as he is Slick has time to bake a cake."

Walter, Slicker and Sweetwater divided up the breakfast onto three tin plates and ate while the rider slowly covered the quarter mile from town to their camp. When he finally arrived, Walter was rolling a cigarette.

"Took you long enough," Walter said as he lit the cigarette.

The man dismounted. "My name is Harmon," he said. "I'm sort of the elected mayor of what will be a town in another year or so."

"I assume you didn't ride out here to watch the sunrise with us," Walter said.

"No, sir, I did not," Harmon said. "The horses have been moved to the tents where the townsfolk stay while the town is under construction. The only people left in town are the hotel manager and his assistant. They'll be watching for you and will hightail it out of there the moment they see you ride in. I'd be obliged if you withheld shooting until they are clear of the fighting."

"We'll do our best," Walter said. "What about the boy?"

"Second floor, back room," Harmon said. "Same room as Beal."

"The gunfighter Russel?" Walter said.

"Second-floor room next to Beal's," Harmon said. "His men are doubled up in rooms on the first and second floors."

"Thirty minutes to sunup," Walter said. "You best go join your people and stay together. If any of you are armed, keep them loaded and ready in case they make a break for their horses. Don't hesitate, just shoot them dead on the spot."

"We're not cowards, you understand," Harmon said. "We're just not gunmen, and we have our womenfolk and kids to think about." Harmon mounted his horse. "Good luck to you all," he said.

"If we make it through this, I'll buy you a drink," Walter said.

"If you make it through this, I'll let you," Harmon said and rode back toward the town at a much faster pace than he arrived.

Walter pulled out his tobacco pouch.

"Sun will be up in thirty minutes," Slicker said.

"Our one advantage will be surprise," Walter said softly. "On horseback, we will dominate, but only for a short while. Once the shooting starts, it will happen quick. Try to put your man down before you dismount and find cover. Don't let them shoot the horse out from under you. Keep firing when you dismount so they can't take careful aim. With lead flying, they won't want to line up in front of you, so try to hit your man on the run and take him down. When your pistol is empty, start right in with your rifle. Whatever cover you find, stay flat on your belly to reload."

Sweetwater suddenly leaned over and vomited. He heaved, gasped and righted himself. "Keep talking, Walter, I'm listening," he said.

"Remember the war?" Walter said. "Once that first shot is fired, it happens so fast, half the time a man doesn't know he's been shot."

"If I get shot, I think I'll know it," Slicker said.

"Me, too," Sweetwater said as he rinsed his mouth with coffee.

"Well, if you do get shot, keep your wits about you," Walter said. "We lost many a man in the war we shouldn't have when they panicked over a flesh wound and exposed themselves only to get shot again."

Slicker nodded and picked up his Henry rifle.

Walter looked at Sweetwater. "Are you ready, Sweet?"

Sweetwater reached for his Winchester. "If I git kilt, Walter, I'm holding you responsible," he said.

"Load all your ammunition into your pockets and let's mount up," Walter said.

CHAPTER FORTY-ONE

Jordan Beal dipped bread into the runny yoke of his fried eggs, put it in his mouth and looked across the table at William. The boy hadn't touched his breakfast. "They cooked it, the least you could do is eat it," Beal said.

William looked down at his untouched plate of fried eggs, bacon and toast, then up at Beal. "What for?" he said. "You're only going to kill me once we arrive in Mexico."

"I told you once and I'll not say it again, nobody is going to kill you," Beal said. "Half is what I want. Half is what's rightly mine. Once I have it, you go free with your half to do with as you please. Now eat your Goddamn breakfast, you stupid spoiled brat. We're leaving in one hour and after that, I don't care if you starve or not."

William picked up his fork and sliced into a fried egg. "I will offer you a deal," he said as he ate the slice.

"A deal?" Beal snorted. "You're just a sniveling child of a boy. What kind of deal can you offer me better than the one I'm making for myself? Why, you can't even stay on your horse more than a mile or two."

"When we reach the next town or a town with a telegraph office, I will wire the attorney in New York and instruct him to give you one-third of my inheritance," William said. "Then you leave me there and ride on and when my uncle shows up, I will ask him not to kill you. A third of my inheritance and your life, that sounds fair to me."

Beal stared at William for several seconds. "You belligerent child," he said. "In the first place, if we did not leave this room it would take your uncle three or four days to reach here, if he is on the right track or even coming."

"He's coming," William said. "Don't worry about that."

"Then let him come," Beal said. "Have you looked at the men we are riding with? They do not scare so easily and pose a mighty sight in their own right."

"Your hired killers won't frighten my uncle," William said. "He is the real thing and you and your killers are not."

"Enough talk," Beal said. "Finish your breakfast."

There was a knock on the door and it opened and William Russel entered the room. A tall, thin, muscular man with black hair and a thick mustache, he had a graceful walk like a cat. Three days' worth of stubble covered his face. He wore a massive .44 Schofield revolver with black ivory grips in a holster on his right hip, and a smaller .38 revolver in a shoulder holster inside his black jacket.

"My men are anxious to ride on," Russel said.

"It's barely daylight," Beal said. "Let me finish breakfast and we'll saddle up. Help yourself to some coffee."

Russel picked up the second china cup from the table and filled it with coffee from the matching pot. He took a sip and walked to the open window to look out. "Not a soul on the street," he remarked.

"Maybe they're late sleepers," Beal said. "Or maybe they're all dead, I don't care which. We got a two-day ride to Alamosa, so make sure we're well supplied before we leave."

"If the people in this town ever wake up and that general store opens," Russel said. He stuck his head out the window to scan the streets below. He turned back around and looked at Beal. "I don't like this. It's too quiet to suit me. I'm going down to check things out."

"Get the horses saddled while you're at it," Beal said. "And if that general store isn't open, open it."

Russel walked out to the street with his two best men, Charlie Blacksmith and Jed Logan. Russel paused on the hotel steps to roll a cigarette and strike a match.

"Not a body around," Russel said.

"Maybe they still asleep in their tents out in the field?" Blacksmith said.

"Maybe," Russel said. "Let's saddle the horses."

"Want me to check around town?" Blacksmith said.

"No."

They walked to the edge of the budding town to the livery where the sliding doors were cracked open.

"Door's open," Logan said.

Russel grabbed the doors and slid them wide open and looked into the empty livery. "Gone," he said. "All of them."

Russel shoved open Beal's hotel room door and entered without knocking. "Problem," Russel said.

Beal stood up from the table. "What?"

"Look out the window, tell me what you see," Russel said.

Beal went to the window. "I see some of your men standing around doing nothing while I pay them for the privilege."

"See any townsfolk about?"

Beal turned around and looked at Russel. "No."

"And you won't see any horses, either," Russel said.

"What are you talking about, Russel?" Beal said.

At the table, William said, "He's talking about my uncle, Mr. Beal."

Beal wagged a finger at William. "You shut up before I smack you," he said.

"The boy could be right," Russel said. "They took our horses and lit out. They definitely put us into a trap on foot."

"We had a hundred-mile lead on that old fool," Beal said. "It's impossible he caught up to us."

"Is it?" Russel said. "The boy slowed us down quite a bit."

"Get the rest of your men and get down there," Beal said. "Find out what the hell is going on around here."

Russel stormed out of the room.

William looked at Beal. "I told you," he said.

Beal lurched at William and smacked the boy hard across the face.

"I told you to shut up," Beal said.

Even though the smack stung and left a red mark on his face, William grinned at Beal.

Russel and his eight men met in the street in front of the hotel.

"What the hell we supposed to do with no horses?" one of the men complained. "Walk outta here?"

"Shut up," Russel said. "Charlie, Jed, come with me to the livery. The rest of you fan out and see if you can find somebody in this craphole town who knows something."

Russel, Blacksmith and Logan turned and walked toward the livery.

The remaining six men fanned out in different directions to check shops and stores along the street.

When Russel, Blacksmith and Logan reached the livery, they entered and walked through the empty building to the opposite end. Russel opened the rear door and looked out. "Charlie, Jed, have a look at this," he said and he stepped outside.

Blacksmith and Logan joined Russel and they looked a hundred yards in the distance where the tents were set up and every horse from the livery, theirs included, was gathered in a close circle, most likely hobbled together.

"What the hell's going on, Will?" Blacksmith said.

"We been set up, that's what's going on," Russel said.

"Should we git our horses?" Logan said.

"Walk out to an open field where a hundred men stand with rifles?" Russel said. "No, we'll stay here and wait."

"For what?" Blacksmith said.

A shot suddenly rang out from the street. Russel drew his .44 Schofield. "For that," he said. "Come on, I believe we have to kill us an old man," he said.

CHAPTER FORTY-TWO

Walter, Slicker and Sweetwater rode their horses slowly across the open field to the newly budding town. The sun was low in the sky and on their backs as they rode past the first building and turned onto the main street.

A man on the plank sidewalk in front of the general store turned and looked at Walter. The man had the hard look of a hired gunman about him and as he reached for his Colt revolver, Walter drew his .45 Colt, cocked it and fired one bullet through the man's chest. The bullet went through his heart and came out his back and the man fell dead on the spot.

Five other men immediately converged on the street, three with Winchester rifles. They opened fire at Walter, Slicker and Sweetwater.

"You done it now!" Slicker shouted to Walter.

Walter, Slicker and Sweetwater returned fire. "Sorry to spoil your peaceful morning, Slick," Walter said. "Next time, I'll let the man just politely shoot me."

"We're sitting ducks here," Slicker said.

"Ride down the street, find cover!" Walter yelled.

They rode ten yards and dismounted with bullets whizzing by their heads. Walter, rifle in hand, threw himself behind a water trough. Slicker and Sweetwater, also with rifles in hands, squeezed into an alley between the general store and post office building to make themselves smaller targets.

Across the street, Russel's five men rushed along the sidewalk and street, firing their weapons as they ran.

Several shots hit the water trough in front of Walter and water ran out of the holes to the dirt street. Walter jumped up quick and fired several shots with his .45 Colt pistol and some of the men scattered for cover.

There was a moment of silence.

Then Walter heard footsteps on a plank sidewalk and peered around the trough to see Russel and two of his men walking along. They stopped across the street in front of the saloon. If there was any fear in Russel, it didn't show in his face.

"Hey, old man!" Russel shouted. "You started a fight you can't win. Best give yourself up or die in the street. Either way, you ain't getting the boy and spoiling my payday and that's all I care about."

"The boy's nothing to you, Russel!" Walter shouted. "This is between family. Bow out and the shooting ends."

"No good, Burke!" Russel shouted. "I'm being paid to do what I do. I always see a job to the end."

Walter looked back at the alley where Slicker and Sweetwater were hiding. Slicker went down on one knee and took aim with his Henry rifle. Standing, Sweetwater aimed his Winchester.

"I'm sorry to hear that, Russel!" Walter shouted.

Russel motioned to Blacksmith and Logan to take cover as he knelt down behind the water trough in front of the saloon.

"This is your call, Burke!" Russel shouted.

"It is at that!" Walter shouted. "So let's get to it!"

In his hotel room, Beal watched the street from his window. "What is he waiting for?" he said. "Kill them."

Behind Beal, William said, "My uncle will. All of them."

"I told you to shut up," Beal said.

"Afraid?" William said.

Beal spun around and punched William in the face, knocking

the boy to the floor. "You're the one who should be afraid," Beal snarled. "Because you'll die first."

Russel aimed his massive Schofield pistol at the trough Walter was hiding behind. He fired one shot and then the shooting began again.

Once it began, there was no turning it back, especially against a man like Burke.

Slicker and Sweetwater fired round after round with their rifles. Walter emptied his pistol, then grabbed his Winchester and began firing that.

Russel's men emptied their weapons.

The first man hit was a Russel man who took a shot in the face with a round from Slicker's Henry rifle. The massive .44-caliber bullet struck the man in his left eye and exited through the back of his skull. There wasn't much of his face or skull left when he hit the ground.

Several of Russel's men concentrated their fire on the alleyway and a bullet struck Slicker in the left side, entering and exiting the exterior wall of his abdomen. It stung hot like a bee sting and a red stain appeared on his shirt. He fell backward and Sweetwater emptied his Winchester to give Slicker time to crawl back into the alley out of the line of fire. As soon as Slicker was clear, Sweetwater raced back into the alley.

"How bad?" Sweetwater said.

"Not bad enough," Slicker said. "Best reload."

On the street, there was a momentary pause while everyone reloaded.

"Slick, how bad you hit!" Walter shouted.

"Enough to get me good and mad," Slicker said as he appeared in the alley and fired a round into a Russel man who was reloading his revolver behind a wood post. The man dropped the revolver and grabbed his right side where the bullet struck and lodged. Slicker took aim and fired another bullet into the man's throat and he fell dead to the wood sidewalk, a bloody mess.

Then Slicker opened up with the Henry rifle as Sweetwater charged out of the alley and jumped to the wood sidewalk behind another water trough. Sweetwater immediately opened fire with his Winchester to give Slicker cover.

As bullets flew by, Slicker jumped out of the alley, turned and threw himself through the plate-glass window of the general store.

Russel motioned for his men to concentrate their fire on Walter and a dozen shots hit the water trough.

Slicker opened fire with his Winchester through the window of the general store to give Walter cover.

Russel jumped up and fired several shots at Slicker in the window and nicked him in the arm. Slicker jumped backward to safety with a red spot on his shirt.

Walter fired at Russel and Russel ducked back down behind the water trough.

Two of Russel's men charged the street, rapid-firing their pistols at Walter, and Sweetwater fired his Winchester and one of them dropped to the street with a belly wound. Slicker fired his Henry rifle from the window and the second man dropped beside the first, gut shot. Neither man was dead and still capable of returning fire, so Slicker took careful aim and killed them both.

Walter turned and saw a Russel man sneaking up on Sweetwater and Walter had to expose himself in order to fire at the Russel man. Walter fired twice, the first bullet striking the man in the left leg, the second in the right lung. The man went down hard and would die slowly, gasping for air as his lungs filled and he drowned in his own blood. As Walter shot the man, Russel took advantage of Walter's momentary exposure and fired upon him, hitting Walter in the upper left leg.

Walter returned fire and threw himself on the ground and rolled closer to the water trough for cover.

Sweetwater came up to fire on Russel and Russel shot Sweetwater in the left side. Sweetwater dropped his Winchester and rolled to the trough and stayed motionless for a moment. Funny how Walter was right, Sweetwater thought. When the bullet struck his left side, it felt like a hot pinch and in the heat of battle a man might not even pay it no mind until it was too late and he bled to death.

Walter opened fire with his Winchester to cover Sweetwater and Russel was forced to retreat behind the water trough.

"Sweet!" Walter yelled as he grabbed his Winchester.

"What?" Sweetwater shouted.

"Slick?" Walter shouted.

"In the general store!" Slicker shouted.

"When I say so, give me cover," Walter said. He reloaded his .45 Colt, then the Winchester rifle. "Hey Russel, the odds are a bit better now, ain't they?"

"But not good enough, old man," Russel said.

"We'll see!" Walter shouted. He turned and shouted, "Now!"

From behind the trough, Sweetwater opened fire with his Winchester. Slicker opened fire with his Henry rifle from the window of the general store. In all, thirty bullets fired across the street.

Russel, Blacksmith, Logan and one other Russel man stayed in cover while the barrage of bullets took out windows, made holes in doors, posts and walls.

After the last bullet hit the wall behind Russel, there was a moment of silence. He, Blacksmith, Logan and the fourth man jumped from their cover to open fire and there in the street was Walter with his Winchester at his hip.

★ ★ ★ ★ ★

From a half mile away, Dodge, Bell and Winslow heard the first echoes of gunfire. They were riding at a quick gate and immediately broke into a flat-out run. Aided by the railroad, they were able to travel eighty miles due southwest and pick up the trail from ranchers who donated horses and stay just a day's ride behind. They rode through the night and picked up the new trail due west and pushed hard to catch Walter and his friends.

Kneeling down at the open window, Beal watched the gunfight unfold on the street below. He didn't hear William arise from the floor and grab the heavy coffee pot from the table until it was too late. Beal spun around just as William swung the pot and smashed Beal in the nose with it, breaking the pot and nose with one blow.

Beal fell backward as blood gushed from his nose. He drew the .32 belly gun from its pocket holster and fired several times at William as the boy ran out the door.

He heard the boy cry out and fall to the hardwood floor.

"Dammit," Beal swore as he stood up.

Russel realized he'd been outfoxed by Walter. The damn old cowboy got the jump on his men and stood his ground on the street and rapid-fired the Winchester. One bullet struck Blacksmith in the shoulder and spun him around to the ground. A second bullet hit Logan in the right hand and he screamed and dropped his Colt revolver to the ground. Walter fired another round and hit Logan in the stomach and he pitched forward to the street. The fourth man fired his revolver and a bullet struck Walter in the left abdomen, passing straight through and into a plate-glass window behind him.

Walter dropped to one knee and emptied the Winchester into

the fourth man's chest, blowing the man backward to the street.

Reloaded, Slicker and Sweetwater jumped out and unleashed a barrage of bullets to give Walter cover and Russel turned and kicked in the saloon door and jumped to the safety of the floor inside.

Slowly, Walter stood up.

Blacksmith rose to his feet with cocked revolver in right hand.

Walter drew his 45 Colt, cocked it and shot Blacksmith in the chest. Blacksmith hit a wood beam behind him, stumbled forward and Walter shot him a second time and Blacksmith pitched forward into the street, dead before he made contact.

Slicker and Sweetwater limped to Walter.

"I'm all shot up," Slicker said.

"I ain't much better," said Sweetwater.

Walter reloaded and holstered his .45 Colt. "You two hens quit your complaining and watch the street," he said. "If I don't come back, gun Russel down and go after the boy. Kill Beal if you have to, but get the boy."

"You going in after him alone?" Slicker said.

"I am," Walter said. "He's got no horse and no place to go."

"You got nothing to prove, Walter," Slicker said. "Not to us."

"This ain't about proving," Walter said. "It's about making things right."

Walter stepped up onto the wood sidewalk and pushed open the saloon doors. Russel was at the bar, peacefully having a drink when Walter walked in and went to the opposite end of the bar.

Russel appeared unbothered by Walter entering the saloon and poured himself another drink. He raised the glass to Walter. "You earned a moment's quarter and a free drink, old man. Pour yourself one of the good stuff."

Walter reached behind the bar for a bottle of rye and a shot glass. He pulled the cork and filled the glass. "Should we drink to our health?" he said.

"My men are dead and I'm out a great deal of money," Russel said. "I wouldn't be truthful if I said I would drink to your health."

"Then let's drink to mutual respect and unfinished business," Walter said and raised the glass with his left hand and downed the shot. He immediately refilled the shot glass.

"The boy said you were a tough old bird who wouldn't go easy," Russel said and downed his shot of whiskey. "Beal wouldn't listen. I told him we should ride into Utah and hide out in the mountains, but he wanted to go to Mexico."

"Beal will be dead shortly," Walter said. "And all this for what, money he didn't earn and has no claim to."

"Money is a funny thing," Russel said. "It will make a man go to lengths he never dreamed of to get enough of it only to find there is not enough to satisfy him."

"True enough words," Walter nodded. He gulped the shot of rye in one quick motion, then gently set the glass on the bar. "Whenever you are ready I will accommodate," he said.

Russel turned to face Walter directly. "You're shot full of holes and even if you weren't, you're no match for me with a handgun," he said. "Not at this close range."

"Maybe not, but you are at a disadvantage," Walter said.

"And what disadvantage is that?" Russel said.

"My Colt is already out," Walter said and squared off against Russel to reveal the cocked .45 Colt revolver in his right hand.

Russel proved himself a lightning-fast draw as he cleared leather and managed to cock his .44 Schofield before Walter shot him in the chest.

The heavy .45 bullet spun Russel around and he crashed into the bar, but wasn't finished. He turned, raised his Schofield and fired wide at Walter just as Walter fired a second shot that hit Russel high in the chest just below the neck and knocked him off his feet to the floor.

Walter holstered the .45 and slowly walked to the fallen gunfighter. Drawing his least breath, Russel looked up at Walter.

"You were too good to face straight up and I'm not about to let the boy die without a chance at life," Walter said.

"You'll kill Beal then?" Russel gasped.

"I will, or my partners will."

"I didn't like him much anyway," Russel said and closed his eyes.

Walter walked back to his shot glass and filled it with rye, turned to Russel, raised the glass and downed the shot.

Slicker and Sweetwater stayed at the ready on the street in front of the saloon. They heard a noise and spun toward the hotel across the street from them. They were shocked to see Jordan Beal walk down the steps of the hotel with William in his arms. The boy was unconscious. A deep red blood stain dripped from the back of the boy's shirt. Beal held a pocket pistol in his left hand to the boy's head.

Beal looked at Slicker and Sweetwater. "I will thank you to throw down your weapons," he said. "Before this boy dies from his wound."

Slicker and Sweetwater didn't move an inch.

Beal cocked the .32 revolver and held it tight against William's forehead. "Go ahead, kill me. I'll take the boy with me," he said. "Stay as you are and he bleeds to death."

Slicker and Sweetwater tossed their rifles to the street.

"Pistols, too," Beal said.

Slicker and Sweetwater pulled their pistols and tossed them in the street next to their rifles.

"Now step up on the sidewalk away from them guns," Beal said.

Slicker and Sweetwater stepped up to the wood sidewalk and

looked at Beal.

"Where is that miserable old man?" Beal said.

Walter stepped out of the saloon with his .45 Colt aimed right at Beal. "Right here, Beal," he said.

"And what do you plan to do, shoot me?"

"If I have to," Walter said.

"Then kill me," Beal said. "But, you'll be killing this boy in the process."

Walter held his aim on Beal. "How much money is enough, Beal?" he said.

"I wasn't greedy," Beal said. "I would have settled for half her estate. I was her husband. I deserved at least that much."

"Deserved?" Walter said. "I believe that fine house more than covered your deserved."

"My business went bad," Beal said. "I needed the money to stay afloat. Joanna knew that before she died. The house doesn't cover half of that."

"Joanna knew exactly what she was doing, you miserable excuse for a man," Walter said.

"Keep talking, Burke," Beal said. "You're talking this boy right into an early grave. I shot him in the back, although I didn't mean to, but that's the way it is. If he doesn't get to a doctor fast, he'll bleed to death. Now put down that gun and get me a horse. I'll ride to Pueblo and get the boy a doctor. Anybody follows me and the boy won't live. I give you all the credit in the world for taking down Russel, now give yourself some credit and be smart. Drop the gun if you want this boy to live."

Walter held his aim for many long seconds and then slowly lowered the .45 Colt and tossed it in the street. "Sweet, Slick, which one of you can walk?" he said.

"I can," Sweetwater said.

"Go out to the field there and return with my horse," Beal

said. "A spotted bay with a black mark on her nose. No tricks, just my horse."

Sweetwater turned and walked through an alleyway toward the field where the townsfolk and horses were gathered.

"Now you two, sit down on the sidewalk there and keep your hands where I can see them," Beal said.

Walter and Slicker sat on the sidewalk and looked at Beal.

"Can I roll a smoke?" Walter said.

"Can you do it with your hands in sight?" Beal said.

Walter lifted his tobacco pouch from his vest pocket and a rolling paper. He started to roll a cigarette. "You told me to be smart," Walter said as he struck a match and lit the cigarette. "What about yourself?"

"What about me?" Beal said.

"Say you keep your word and take the boy to a doctor," Walter said. "Even if he lives, do you think I'll forget about this? I will hunt you down and kill you if it takes the rest of my natural life. I feel you should know that just to be fair."

"What do you propose?" Beal said. "That I kill the three of you before I ride out?"

"In your place, I would," Walter said as he blew smoke. "Unless self-preservation is a quality you don't possess."

"Nice try, old man," Beal said. "But, for me to kill even one of you I have to release the boy. I may kill one, but not two. And then there is your third man to worry about. No, I think I'll just wait for the horse."

"Suit yourself," Walter said.

Slicker rode in on Beal's large bay and immediately dismounted.

"That's the one," Beal said. "Now all three of you walk to the end of the street far away from your guns."

Walter and Slicker stood up. "I'll see you soon, Beal," Walter said.

Sweetwater joined Walter and Slicker and they walked to the end of the street some fifty feet from Beal.

Beal stuck the .32 revolver in his belt, placed William over the saddle, then mounted the bay. "You'll find the boy at the doctor's in Pueblo," he said and rode off southwest out of town.

Walter, Slicker and Sweetwater rushed to their guns, but before they could pick them up, Dodge, Bell and Winslow rode in from the north side of town and quickly dismounted.

"You three?" Walter said.

"We've been tracking you for days," Dodge said. "Rode through the night to catch you. We felt we owed you something."

"We saw what happened," Bell said. "We didn't want to risk the boy's life showing ourselves."

"I appreciate your concern, but the boy is shot in the back and bleeding to death," Walter said. "And Beal will kill him if we try to stop him."

"The hell he will," Dodge said and removed his rifle from the saddle. It was a high-powered military rifle with a scope mounted on it, the kind used by snipers. He walked to the street where Beal rode out of and to the edge of the open field.

Walter, Slicker, Sweetwater, Bell and Winslow followed Dodge.

"He's four hundred yards downwind already," Slicker said.

Dodge checked the scope and went prone on the grass. "I know it," he said.

"You won't get a second shot," Slicker said.

"I won't need one," Dodge said.

Dodge peered through the scope and lined up the crosshairs with the back of Beal's head. He held his breath and placed his finger on the trigger. With a gentle squeeze, he pulled the trigger.

The shot was loud. About one full second after the report of the round, Beal slumped forward on the bay, then fell off her to the ground. With William prone on the saddle, the bay ran for a few yards, then slowly came to a stop as William fell off the saddle and landed beside the still horse.

Walter turned and started to walk back to where he left his horse. Slicker placed his hand on Walter's arm.

"Even if I had no legs, you couldn't outride me," Slicker said.

Walter turned and looked at Slicker's wounds. "You're bleeding pretty bad yourself," he said.

"I got enough blood in me for one last ride," Slicker said.

"Sweet, get Slick's horse," Walter said.

Sweetwater turned and walked down to the end of the street where the horses had gathered once the shooting stopped.

Dodge stood up and dusted off his pants. "Let's get our horses," he said.

"You'll never keep up with me," Slicker said.

"No, but we can put the boy on your saddle and follow you," Dodge said. "If you fall, we'll take over."

Sweetwater returned with Slicker's horse.

"Help me up," Slicker said.

Walter gave Slicker a boost into the saddle. Immediately, Slicker rode out to the field where William lay beside Beal's horse.

Dodge, Winslow and Bell mounted up and followed Slicker.

Walter and Sweetwater watched as Slicker reached William and dismounted. Dodge, Winslow and Bell reached Slicker a few seconds later. Winslow and Bell dismounted and lifted William onto Slicker's saddle. Then they lifted Slicker back onto the saddle and with a jerk, he was off and running.

Winslow and Bell remounted and with Dodge, they raced off behind Slicker.

"Nothing to do now except say a prayer," Walter said as he watched them race away into the distance.

"I don't know any," Sweetwater said.

"Make one up," Walter said. "And it doesn't have to rhyme either."

Noise behind them caused Walter and Sweetwater to turn around. Harmon and the townsfolk had returned from the field.

"They're all dead," Harmon said. "You killed everybody."

"Those that had it coming," Walter said. "Sorry about shooting your town up. I'll pay for the repairs of what we shot up."

"We have enough supplies on hand all it will cost is some labor," Harmon said.

"I could use a drink," Sweetwater said.

"Let's both have one," Walter said.

"Where's the gunfighter?" Harmon said.

"Dead on the saloon floor," Walter said.

"You men are bleeding, too," Harmon said.

"You got anybody who done some doctoring?" Walter said.

"The hotel manager used to be a dentist back east," Harmon said.

"Get him," Walter said. "We got some wounds need tending. If he ain't squeamish, we'll be having our drink with the gunfighter in the saloon."

CHAPTER FORTY-THREE

Slicker rode his horse with everything the animal had in him, and then he asked it for more. The animal gave him more, all that it had. Flaring its nostrils to take in massive amounts of air, it started to sweat after several miles of hard riding.

After a while, Slicker could no longer hear the three horses behind him. He wasn't sure if it was because they were now too far behind to hear them, or the loss of blood so weakened him, his hearing went dull.

The horse pushed on and thick clumps of lathery sweat flew from its sides and neck. It became a question of who would give out first, the horse or himself, Slicker reasoned and if he had to bet, it would be on himself going before the horse.

The miles passed before him. He knew the boy was alive because every so often, he would groan when bumped around on the saddle. Knowing the boy was still alive made him draw on what little reserve strength he had left, and he called upon his horse to do the same.

The horse, sensing it was life or death, responded and gave Slicker more.

Then things started to go dim in his head and everything around him appeared to slow to a crawl. Slicker knew it was the heavy loss of blood. He put his head down against the horse's neck.

"I need you to get us there," Slicker said. "Or die trying."

As if the horse understood Slicker's words, it found the

strength to go faster, and as it jumped a prairie dog hole, William grunted in pain, telling Slicker and the horse he was still with them.

Another mile passed. Slicker felt what little remaining strength he had start to fade badly. Darkness fell upon him like a warm blanket. He could see stars in the sky even though it was barely ten in the morning.

He rode on.

And the darkness lifted and before him, Slicker could see the ranch he, Walter and Sweetwater spent so many years trying to build. The house was made of logs, with a stone chimney, a corral in front for training horses and a wide open range with good water for grazing. It was exactly as he always thought it would be, beautiful and green.

And theirs.

He rode on and it started to snow. Giant white flakes, perfect and gleaming in the sunlight. Funny, he wasn't cold and the snow wasn't wet. Just pretty.

His hearing faded until all he could hear was the hard, slow breathing of his horse.

And time slowed before his eyes. The ground below him moved at a snail's pace, and Slicker knew he reached the end of it.

Then the sky fell and the ground rose up and everything went warm and dark.

Dodge, Winslow and Bell rode hard, but the gap between them and Slicker widened quickly and a half mile separated them within minutes. Undaunted, they rode on and even though they lost sight of Slicker, they knew the direction he was traveling in, so they weren't worried they would lose his trail.

Then, suddenly, Slicker's horse came into view on the horizon.

"He's slowed down," Winslow shouted.

"No, he isn't moving," Bell shouted.

They pounded their horses and closed the gap to five hundred yards and there, less than a hundred yards in front of Slicker's horse, was the fringe of Pueblo. They kicked the horses for more speed and as the seconds ticked by, they saw the boy was still on the horse.

Bell arrived first and leapt from his horse to the ground where Slicker's horse was peacefully grazing on sweet grass. The horse snorted a bit, but Bell took the reins and calmed it down enough for him to check the boy.

Dodge and Winslow, a fraction behind Bell, jumped from their horses and raced to Slicker on the ground. Dodge rolled him over and checked Slicker's pulse and breath.

"He's alive," Dodge said.

"So is the boy," Bell said.

Dodge looked at Pueblo just a hundred yards in front of them. "What are you standing around for, let's get them to the doctor," he said.

CHAPTER FORTY-FOUR

Walter and Sweetwater rode a buckboard wagon into Pueblo shortly before sundown, using their own horses to tow the wagon. The dentist did a fine job patching their wounds, but they were in no condition to ride a saddle, so they borrowed the wagon from Harmon with a promise to return it intact.

The doctor's office occupied a large, two-story building made of red brick on the north side of town. The doctor's name was Roberts and he was from Boston. He had the latest equipment and drugs available in medicine and even had a telegraph right on his desk to confer with colleagues around the country.

Roberts wore a white coat and a listening device around his neck he called a stethoscope. "It was very close for your friend Mr. Johnson," Roberts said in a funny eastern dude accent when he escorted Walter and Sweetwater to the recovery room. "He lost forty percent of his blood and would not have survived the surgery if not for townspeople donating their blood."

"Donating their blood?" Walter said. "You mean take blood from one person and give it to another?"

"That's exactly what I mean," Roberts said. "And in this case, several people, for both your friend and the boy. The Pinkerton men were first on line to donate. I thought you should know that."

"They're good men, doc," Walter said.

"Don't tell me that, tell them," Roberts said.

They reached the recovery room and Roberts opened the

door. "He may be awake, but I ask you to stay only a moment," Roberts said. "He's still weak and needs rest. The boy is next door. I'll be with him when you're finished with Mr. Johnson."

Walter and Sweetwater entered the room where Slicker was asleep in bed, under the covers. He seemed pale and gaunt, but his breathing appeared normal enough and when Walter whispered his name, Slicker opened his eyes.

"The boy?" Slicker whispered.

"He made it and so did you," Walter said.

Slicker drew in a soft breath. "Being your friend is a pain in the ass sometimes, Walter," he said softly.

"I've been telling him that very thing," Sweetwater said and smiled.

Slicker nodded his head slightly. "Can we git our ranch now?" he whispered.

"I think that would be well advised," Walter said.

Slicker closed his eyes and fell back asleep. Walter and Sweetwater left the room and went next door where Roberts was listening to William's heart with the stethoscope device.

"The boy is still out from the anesthesia," Roberts said. "The bullet went through his upper back, but missed the lungs. His body went into shock, which slowed down his heart and saved his life. I expect him to make a full recovery in time."

"What do I owe you for your work?" Walter said.

"The three Pinkerton men that carried them in paid the bill," Roberts said.

Walter and Sweetwater exchanged glances.

"Now wait a . . ." Walter said.

"They said you would argue, but to tell you it's no use," Roberts said. "They said to tell you they wanted to pay what they owe. They said you'd understand."

Walter nodded.

"The boy needs rest now," Roberts said.

"Say, doc," Walter said. "We got shot up ourselves and a dentist fixed us up. Maybe you could take a look at his work for us?"

"Go down the hall and see my nurse," Roberts said. "She'll take you to an examination room. Remove all your clothes and I'll be there in a moment."

"All?" Sweetwater said.

"Right down to your bare skin," Roberts said.

Walter and Sweetwater caught up with the three Pinkerton detectives in the saloon where they were having a quiet drink.

"The doc said you paid the boy's bill," Walter said. "Our friend, too. And gave them your blood."

"We felt we owed you," Dodge said. "Seeing as how we delivered the boy to Beal in the first place."

"For what it's worth, you set things right and then some," Walter said. "We're grateful to all three of you."

"Sit and have a drink with us," Bell said. He picked up the bottle and filled two empty shot glasses on the tray the bartender brought earlier. "It's something called Jack Daniels."

"It's the least we could do," Walter said.

The five men lifted their glasses and downed the shots.

"Well, we best get back to the doc's," Walter said. "You men take care."

"You do the same," Dodge said. "And if you're ever in need of our services, wire us in Philadelphia."

CHAPTER FORTY-FIVE

Winter 1886

The valley just south of the Eastern Rockies in Wyoming Territory was about the prettiest country a man could ever hope to see in his lifetime and the perfect place to start a new ranch.

After buying one thousand acres of land, there was enough cash on hand to purchase timber and logs and the furnishings to build a five-bedroom ranch house, barn, corral and stables.

With William's help, Walter, Slicker and Sweetwater did the bulk of the work themselves. Walter used the remaining expense money to buy two hundred and fifty head of cattle and a dozen horses. Any additional horses they might need, they could pick up wild ones off the prairie and tame in the corral. They already had orders from the Army outposts for mounts and the extra cash would come in handy while they raised the cattle for beef back east.

A gentle snow began to fall as Walter and Sweetwater watched Slicker teach William how to make a horse prance inside the corral. With a rope tied to the reins and Slicker holding the rope, the horse could only ride in circles. William sat in the saddle as the horse marched in a quick-step cadence that made the horse appear to prance.

"I can't do that, Walt," Sweetwater said. "Can you do that?"

"Slick tried to teach me once, but all I did was make the horse throw a shoe," Walter said. "And me along with it."

"The boy looks good," Sweetwater said. "Filled out some, too."

"He's fourteen now," Walter said. "Almost a man."

"What about the boy's schooling?" Sweetwater asked.

"I know it," Walter said. "Soon as spring arrives, I'll take him by train to San Francisco. Let him have some fun before he returns to the books."

A bell sounded from inside the house, announcing that breakfast was ready and on the table.

"Slick, you and the boy come on now," Walter said. "That old fool we got for a cook gets awful upset if you're late to the table."

"Say, Walt, seeing as how it looks like snow is on the way, I think I'll take a ride into town for supplies," Sweetwater said.

"And see that nice-looking woman with the gold hair who runs the general store in the process," Walter said.

"Ah, leave him be," Slicker said as he opened the gate. "It won't do you no harm to take a wife, you know. Mellow out that miserable hide of yours. And it's called blonde, not gold."

"I am nagged enough by you two," Walter said. "A wife would just finish the job of putting me to an early grave. William, get in the house before the old goat blows his top. I'll be along directly."

Walter turned and walked toward the barn to the right of the corral.

"My uncle is getting married?" William said to Slicker.

"Sure," Sweetwater said. "The day that pigs give cow milk."

Walter walked around the side of the barn to the small fenced-in cemetery he built right after the house. There was one headstone. He opened the gate, entered and stood in front of it. The inscription read simply, Joanna Burke. 1846–1885. Wife. Mother. Sister.

"Well, Jo," Walter said. "He'll be a fine man soon enough. You

246

should be proud of the son you raised."

As the snow started to fall a bit heavier, Walter rolled a cigarette and lit it with a wood match. A month after buying the property, he wired the lawyer in New York and requested to have Joanna's body moved to Wyoming. There were some papers to sign, a judge to speak with, but the lawyer got permission and her coffin arrived by train. It was a comfort knowing she rested nearby.

Walter inhaled on the cigarette and blew smoke that was quickly lost in the falling snow. He knew soon Sweetwater would marry that shopkeeper and that was a good thing. There was a nice patch of land on the south side of the ranch for a big house and seeing as how the woman was but thirty, a bunch of kids to fill the rooms. Walter already set aside money for timber and supplies, as did Slicker.

In the background, Walter heard the bell ring again. He tossed the cigarette into the snow and walked back to the house.

Walter opened the door and Duffy immediately said, "Wipe your feet, Walter. This isn't the saloon in Denver here."

Walter wiped his boots on the floor mat. "Duffy," he said. "I'm starting to feel regret at having them Pinkerton boys find you back east."

"We'll talk about it over breakfast," Duffy said.

As Walter and Duffy entered the vast kitchen, Walter removed his hat and gently tossed it onto the walnut grain box phone mounted on the wall. As Walter sat at the table, Slicker said, "Why'd you want that thing for, Walt? It will be ten years before they have telephone lines strung in these parts."

"I know," Walter said as he dug into the bowl of scrambled eggs on the table. "I just want to be ready when they get here."

ABOUT THE AUTHOR

Although born in New York City, **Ethan J. Wolfe** began a fascination with the Old West as a child and studied the western culture, myths and history all his life. He has traveled the west and visited many of the sights and locations made famous in western folklore. *The Last Ride* is his first western novel, the first of many more to follow.